PIPPA GOODHART

RAVEN BOY

Catnip

CATNIP BOOKS
Published by Catnip Publishing Ltd.
Islington Business Centre
3-5 Islington High Street
London N1 9LQ

First published 2007
1 3 5 7 9 10 8 6 4 2

A CIP catalogue record for this book is available from the
British Library

ISBN 978-1-84647-025-7

Printed in Poland

www.catnippublishing.co.uk

For my Mary, with love

Contents

In a tight-packed house fug-full of sleeping people, their smells and their snores and shouts, a tall boy tipped out of bed and climbed up into the attic to throw open the casement to lean out and breathe in the cooler air from outside. Nick looked up from the dark crowded lane cramped with homes, up to the moon-silvered sky where the ravens were flying. In the daytime those birds flew and worked alone. But on hot summer nights they swarmed together and flew in circles, like dancers, thought Nick. Or like witches, casting spells. They writhed and whirled up and up over their Tower-of-London home, and Nick watched them and wondered. Seth had told him that there had almost always been ravens at the Tower, always for hundreds of years until the people of England cut off their king's head. When that king went, so too did the ravens, and they didn't return until the new king came to the throne. Why had the birds stayed away just then, wondered Nick. And why did they ever come back? If he was a raven he would fly away and away and never come back.

Chapter One

London was hot. So hot that the air shimmered like water. Even the flies buzzing over the stinking rubbish in the lane seemed to buzz more lazily than usual. Seth Binder wiped a rag over his damp forehead as he stood in the doorway of the timber and wattle house. He called out,

'Are you coming, Nick? Do you want a day's work or not?'

There were muffled thumps and noises within the cramped darkness inside, and at last a skinny, dark-haired boy came clattering down the stairs. He was frowning.

'What's up?' asked Seth.

'Mother,' said Nick. 'She fell and she has a headache and she's hot …'

'We're all hot!' laughed Seth. 'And we'll get even hotter as the day goes on, so hurry up and let's get going before we bake in the midday sun.'

There were sounds from up above – moans

and another thump – and Nick and Seth glanced upward. Seth's laughter stopped.

'You don't think it might be the plague, do you, Nick? There's more dying of it every day, they say. We've nailed up a family in Fenchurch Street now and I saw a man yesterday fall where he stood, and none to help him. You don't think …' He took a step back from the doorway and put a hand over his mouth to block out the smelly fug of the house. Mistress Jenkins came bustling down the stairs, pinning up her hair as she came. She cuffed Nick over the head as she swept past him and raised a wagging finger at the man in the doorway.

'What's this talk of plague, Seth Binder? In my house? Never! And don't you go spreading any such gossip!' She turned to Nick. 'Best way you can help your mother is to go and earn a day's wages to put towards the rent. It's worry that's making her ill, I'm sure of it. Now, take a bite of lunch with you, and go.'

'But what about Mercy?' asked Nick.

'I'll keep your sister from bothering your mother, if that's what's on your mind. Your mother needs rest. Mercy can be of use to me down here. She can take the stones from the raisins ready for the baking. She'll like that.' Mistress Jenkins reached over the wooden table and dipped a hand into the bread crock. She tore off a hunk of bread which she wrapped hastily in a cloth and handed to Nick to push into his pouch. 'Now go off out with Master Binder, Nicholas Truelove. And I want to hear of no idle gossip from either of you concerning illness at my boarding house, if you please. It's hard enough to find lodgers in these troubled times.'

So Nick stepped out from the indoor smells of washing soaking and overnight piss pots, and into the lane.

'You can carry this,' said Seth, so Nick took the heavy bundle of tools and followed Seth downhill, dodging over dusty rubbish that needed a good rain shower to flush the lane clean.

'Where's the job?' asked Nick.

'A repair at Tower Wharf,' said Seth. 'The tide's out so the timbers should be high and dry.'

Good, thought Nick. He liked the broad brown silky river and the boats that came and went on it carrying goods and people. But there was something next to the river that Nick did not like. As they walked nearer, Nick looked up at the great Tower of London that rose up with a mass of towers pointing skywards within great stone walls.

That walled and moated fortress was the place that held the King's power. It was where the King kept his jewels and his weapons, his soldiers and his prisoners. It was where they had taken Father.

The press men had taken Nick's father one night as he was out delivering a pair of gloves to a gentleman customer. They had taken Father to the Tower in chains and forced him to become a sailor on one of the King's warships. Then they had sent Father out to sea in a ship to be fired at by Dutch cannons so that the ship burnt and sank and Father never came home again. Nick clenched his fists. The King is a murderer, he thought. The King killed Father, and he took our home too, and my life. Because they'd had to leave their home, without Father to earn their living. Nick had had to leave his school and take work where he could, usually with parish carpenter, Seth Binder.

'Stop moon-beaming and concentrate,' said Seth. 'See that broken spar there? We need to cut out the rotten part and splice in a new piece of oak.'

'Then we'll want the saw, won't we?' asked Nick, opening out the roll of tools.

'That's it,' said Seth. 'Now, you get down into that mud. Don't look at me like that, boy. It'll be lovely and cool between your toes! Now, grab your end of the saw. Wrap a leather round your hand as I've shown you before. Your hands are as soft as a baby's.'

'They are not!'

'Use the leather!' said Seth.

The sawing did make Nick's hands sore, and his feet stuck in the thick stony mud, and his back ached. But there was a satisfaction in sawing back and forth with Seth, cutting away the rotten timber ready to replace it with new. Then Nick climbed out of the mud to work on the new wood, and he was glad of the mud's cooling dampness on his legs in the hot sunshine. Beside him, the river slap-slopped and in the distance there were the sounds of boats and shouting and horses on cobbles and the great water wheel churning under the bridge. Seth pared at a corner of the wood with a knife in the same way that Mother would pare a turnip for the pot. Nick whittled pegs to fix the wood in place.

As the sun rose high overhead, Seth went to quench his thirst in the ale-house, leaving Nick with the lunch in his pouch. He sat beside a mooring post and watched two seagulls having a tug-of-war over a scrap of fish. Their screeching meant that they opened their beaks and dropped the fish, and while they flapped furiously at each other, a big black raven scrambled across and pinched the fish from beside their feet. Nick laughed.

'You! Boy there! Take the rope!' shouted a gentleman's voice from the river. 'Quickly, boy! Gracious, have the young no respect for their betters these days?'

A rope hit Nick around the head, and he reached out and took it as a silk-stockinged foot in a fine buckled shoe stepped onto the quay. Nick jumped up and bowed his head a little as a grand figure stepped from the rowing boat that had slipped so silently alongside the wharf. As Nick straightened up again, he saw the gentleman from feet upwards. Plum-coloured silk stockings went up into frilled breeches and a stomach as plump as a pillow wrapped around with a wine-coloured velvet coat worked with golden stitched flowers. It was a very fine coat, but it was making the gentleman hot, and so was the big grey wig that tumbled curls around the gentleman's fatly sneering face. Nick looked the gentleman straight in the eye and he didn't blink.

'Insolence!' said the gentleman, and he turned and waddled towards the entrance to the Tower.

Nick knew who the grand man was. He was Sir John Robinson, Lord Lieutenant of His Majesty's Tower of London, and in charge of prisoners and pressed men taken on the King's orders. Nick would like to capture the King and send *him* into the Tower to be tortured or sent out to the great deep lonely sea to be shot at and drowned. Nick gathered phlegm in his mouth and he spat it towards the back of that grand man who did the King's dirty work.

Then Nick took the bread from his pouch. He chewed it moodily and scowled after Sir John Robinson as he went within the great walls of the Tower. But something sharp suddenly attacked Nick's bare leg.

'Hey!'

Nick hopped backwards, dropping the bread from his hand. A big black raven tweaked up the bread in its beak, tipped back its head and swallowed.

'You thieving devil!' said Nick, part angry, part amused. The raven had a distinctive tuft of feathers standing up from its head. It was a young raven, not yet fully grown. It was the same raven that had taken the fish from the seagulls. 'You've robbed my lunch!' said Nick.

But the bird had brought payment for the meal. It had dropped something small and shiny and circular onto the dusty quayside before snatching Nick's bread. Now Nick bent and picked the thing up. It was a button. Nick looked at the raven, its head on one side and its eyes shining back at Nick. 'Where did you get this from?' asked Nick.

'Kraack!'

'From that gentleman who passed by just now?' Nick grinned. He spat on the button and rubbed it clean on his shirt. 'Silver!' The button had a shape of flowers standing proud on the surface. Nick glanced around to check that nobody was watching, then he slipped the button into his breeches pocket.

'I'm not the thief here,' he told the bird. 'You've done the robbery. I'm just accepting your payment.' The raven blinked slowly.

The bird stayed beside Nick and watched as he got back to work, whittling pegs. The raven's head nodded, following each strike of the knife as Nick shaped the peg to fit the hole. 'Is it the shine of it that you like?' asked Nick. 'Well, you can't have the knife, you know. It belongs to Seth.'

'It certainly does. Give it back to me please, Master Nick.'

Seth had beery breath and was in a good mood. He nodded in the direction of the raven. 'Daft bird,' he said.

'He's not daft, he's clever,' said Nick.

'Oh, yes? Horrible birds, ravens; they live their lives by feeding off others. They're parasites, that's what they are. Very devils. They'll have your eyes out, given half a chance. You must've seen them following the death carts and pecking at corpses.' Seth made a face. 'I hate them.'

'That's no worse than how the King lives,' said Nick. 'He takes from others, even their lives sometimes.'

Seth put a hasty finger to his mouth. 'You hush, Nick! That's dangerous talk, especially in an open place like this where there's people that can hear you. And next to the King's own Tower! I know how you feel about what happened to your father, but there's no happiness to be found in hating the King for that. Best settle for life the way that it is. We've all of us had our hardships, and we'll no doubt have more before we're finished. Now, are we going to get this job done or not?' Seth took the peg that Nick had shaped, looked at it critically, then began to hammer it into place.

Nick watched the big bird lift his wings and rise

up into the air, up and away from the hot quayside. The air must be cooler higher up, thought Nick; cool and fresh as country stream water. Nick sighed and picked up the plane to shave the tops of the pegs level with the wharf.

'I wish I was a raven,' said Nick.

'What nonsense are you talking now?' asked Seth. Nick didn't answer, but he thought how wonderful it would be to be able to fly away from life in London's streets whenever he chose.

Chapter Two

When Nick got back to the boarding house in Farthing Lane, Mistress Jenkins opened the door, looked up and down the lane, then pulled Nick inside. She slammed the door shut and spoke close into Nick's face. 'Your mother, Nicholas! She's bad, writhing and moaning and vomiting and talking nonsense and I hardly dare let myself think what I am thinking!'

'And what are you thinking?' asked Nick, although he knew.

'I fear that the you-know-what has come amongst us at last, Nicholas. The plague into my own house!' said Mistress Jenkins. 'I want your mother out of this place, and nobody to know of it, or they'll come and nail us all in to die of it. You must take your mother away from here, Nicholas! I beg you!'

'Take her where?'

'Anywhere! Away! To the Pest House, I suppose.'

'No!'

Nick wrenched himself free of Mistress Jenkins's bony grasp and he ran up the stairs to his Mother. He opened the door to the small room that they rented. Then he stopped still, halted by the sounds and smells from within. He took a deep breath, and stepped towards the bed.

'Mother?' asked Nick almost shyly. The woman who lay in front of him didn't seem to be the same mother he knew so well. Her pink face with hair neatly tucked into a crisp white cap had become pale and wild. It was so tight with pain that Nick could see the skull very near the surface of her skin. She was grey as dough. Her brown hair was crumpled around her head, her body twisted in sheets wet with sweat. Nick reached out a hand and he touched his mother's forehead. It was clammy chill. Mother smelt foul and Nick didn't like to breathe near her. But his mother's pale bony hand suddenly wavered up towards him. Nick took it.

'Mother?'

'Nic…' began his mother, but the effort to form his name was too much.

'Yes, Mother?' he whispered.

'Mer...'

'Mercy, yes? I shall care for her always, Mother. I promise it.'

But Nick's mother wanted to say more.

'Yes?' whispered Nick.

'Bury her.' Mother's eyes were wild, but her speech suddenly clear. 'Bury Mercy. With me.'

'No!' Nick flung down his mother's hand. He looked to the doorway and saw his small sister standing there, shaking and big-eyed with the thought of being put into a hole in the ground together with the corpse of their mother, covered with soil until there was only darkness and no air and... Nick went and pulled Mercy to him and held her tight. 'Don't you fear, Mercy. I shall keep you safe.'

'Oh, Nicholas!' Mistress Jenkins was on the staircase, wailing her fear, scared to get close to the illness but too afraid of sickness to ignore it. 'We have to know for sure. Pull back your mother's shift and take a look for the signs of plague, and I pray it won't be there!'

Nick swallowed. 'I will, but only if you take Mercy downstairs and away from here. Only if...'

Mistress Jenkins was suddenly angry, finger pointing. 'You are in no position to tell me what to do in my own house, young man.'

'Oh?' said Nick, fierce back. 'Then shall I shout up the stairs to Mr Trenter and the Webber family? Shall I open the window and shout into the lane that this house is a plague house?'

'No, Nicholas!' Mistress Jenkins's hands shuddered either side of her cheeks. 'Oh, you mustn't, I beg you! I shall take Mercy down directly.'

Nick gently pushed Mercy out through the door, and the old woman led her down the stairs.

Nick closed his eyes. Please God, he thought, let us all be mistaken and it isn't the plague after all. He turned his head away from his mother and took a breath. Then he turned back and pulled open the damp neck of Mother's nightgown. Nothing to see. Nick bit his lip. He tugged the gown down over Mother's right shoulder. And there it was; a great purple swelling blooming under the armpit. Nick felt his stomach heave. His heart was thumping in his ears. 'Oh, dear God!'

His mother moaned, and Nick fled, wiping and wiping his hands on his breeches as he went.

Nick went to the kitchen where Mistress Jenkins was on her knees, praying.

'Good Lord have mercy...'

Nick looked at his small sister, crumpled in

a corner and with her hands over her ears. She looked frail as paper. Nick knew she hadn't the strength to survive if the plague ever got into her.

'Mercy,' he said gently, pulling her hands away from her ears. 'We shall go from here.'

Mercy looked up at him. 'But, what of Mother?'

'Mother is gone from us,' said Nick, and Mercy's eyes and mouth opened big in her white face. 'We must go.' He quickly snatched a hunk of bread from a plate on the table and the left-over mutton on a bone that sat in a bowl, and he wrapped them all in a cloth left drying by the fire. He checked that he had his knife safe on a cord from his waist.

'What are you doing, Nicholas?' Mistress Jenkins struggled to her feet. 'That's my food. You cannot leave me with your mother! Nicholas!'

Nick took Mercy's hand. But Mistress Jenkins grabbed hold of Mercy's other arm. 'Don't go, Nicholas! Don't leave me with your mother up there!'

'Let her go!' said Nick fiercely. He tugged Mercy free of the woman, then opened the door and hurried out into the lane, pushing a protesting Mercy before him.

There were people in the lane, two women standing and talking, but they stepped back into their homes as Nick and Mercy ran by. They already know, thought Nick. They'll gossip it up and down the lanes and it won't be long before somebody calls for the searcher to come, and then nobody can escape.

'Nick? Where are we going?'

'Away,' said Nick.

'Where?' sobbed Mercy. 'Nick!'

'Shush!' Nick wished he knew where to go. At the end of the lane he stopped. The sound of Mother's moans filled his head so that he couldn't think.

'I want to go home!' said Mercy.

Home; where Mother lay dying. Where the searcher would come in his long black gown and bird-head mask to swoop up the stairs and loom over Mother and summon the death cart and the men with long hooked poles. Nick swallowed something that heaved up inside him. He had seen the next bit happen to a neighbour. The body tossed onto a cart full of bodies that had been people. The flies buzzing. The smell. No prayer or headstone to mark the dead person thrown into a plague pit like any other rubbish. Nick clenched

Mercy's small hand tight. They would nail tight shut the door to Mistress Jenkins's house. They would seal everyone inside for forty days and nights and the likelihood was that plague would take them all.

'Run!' Nick hauled Mercy through the lanes and away from that horror.

That was how it had been for London's people for the last two years – people dying and the city dying with them. There was grass along the streets now. Few shops were open, few stalls set up or counters put down. Few physicians or churchmen were left in the city to care for the sick. Those who could had fled. Hardly any of the grand people were left.

That thought suddenly gave Nick an idea of where he could take Mercy to keep her safe. The great houses belonging to the rich people who had gone must be empty. Nick smiled down at Mercy. 'I'll take you to a place that you'll like very much,' he told her.

He hurried her along the narrow lanes shaded by the overhanging storeys of the houses on either side. They left the looming Tower and Farthing Lane and Mother far behind them as they went westwards, towards the setting sun. They hurried past St Paul's and along The Strand, to streets where the evening sun cast big shadows from grand houses sitting within walled gardens.

'We'll live in one of these places,' Nick told Mercy.

'But we've not been invited!' said Mercy. 'And my face is dirty. Mother wouldn't…'

'We won't go in through a front door, nor even through the servants' entrance,' said Nick. 'No one will see whether we are dirty or clean. We'll set up home in secret. Here.' Nick dodged down an alley-way that ran beside one big house. There were shutters over all the windows as if the house was asleep and had its eyes closed. 'Now, hush and do as I say.' Nick looked over his shoulder to check that nobody was watching. Then he jumped up to grab and pull himself up to sit astride the wall.

'Now reach up, Mercy. I'm going to pull you over.'

Mercy was only six years old and slight. Nick, at twelve, could easily lift her. For a moment they perched on the wall like two clumsy birds holding on tight and looking all around.

'Oh!' whispered Mercy, looking at the garden. 'It's like the Garden of Eden from the Bible!'

The garden had apple and plum trees with some

fruit still on them. There were beds of the last of the summer's roses.

'Oh, look, Nick!' whispered Mercy. There was a gardener with a rake in this garden too.

'Get down!' whispered Nick, ducking and pushing Mercy low on the wall. He twisted and dropped quietly down into the garden to crouch behind a quince, then watched and waited until he was sure that the gardener had turned his back before he reached up to take Mercy from the wall. She was trembling. 'Don't fear,' he whispered. 'The house will be empty and all ours.'

Chapter Three

They crept along the walled edge of the garden, watching the gardener and being careful about where their own long evening shadows fell. At times they halted statue-still, then scuttled on towards the house. 'Like playing Grandmother's footsteps,' said Mercy.

'Will you hush?' Nick frowned and put a finger to his lips.

The doors of the great stone house were locked and the windows bolted at their shutters, but Nick found an opening that wasn't secured. Low down and near to the servants' entrance there was a wide low, double door that opened outwards. 'It's the cellar,' said Nick. He peered down into the musty darkness. 'Hold on to my hands, Mercy, and I'll drop you down.'

'But it's dark down there!'

'There will be a way up into the house from it. Come on, quick before that gardener comes round the corner.'

So Nick lowered Mercy into the hole, then dropped down himself, pulling the door flap closed over him. Mercy's hands clung to him, pinch-tight. As their eyes adjusted to the gloom, they could see a little of where they were. The cellar was a low-ceilinged cave of a place, piled with wine bottles and coal, draped with cobwebs and full to the brim with darkness and musty smells.

'It's too dark,' said Mercy.

'It's almost night and night-times should be dark,' said Nick. 'I'm going to look for the trap door.'

'But ...'

'Oh, shush, Mercy! We have to stay somewhere, don't we? Or do you want the watchmen to catch us in the street and send us back to be shut into Mistress Jenkins's house?'

A sudden bump-bump noise came from somewhere up above. 'Ghosts!' said Mercy, her hand to her mouth, and Nick felt a cold shiver down his own back.

'Silly,' he said, but the noise did sound very like a ghost and Nick's voice shook. He thought of Mother in her white night gown, dying. That clammy hand of a thought grabbed him around the neck. Might Mother come in death to find him, to ask Nick why he had left her to die alone? There was a sharp scraping sound and a sudden loud thump above them, and Mercy crouched back in fear.

'They're cutting off somebody's head!' she whispered. 'I heard it fall!' But Nick had heard another sound now, the clink of a knife on a pewter plate. He hugged around Mercy's shoulders.

'Hush now,' he whispered. 'It's a servant up in the kitchen and eating his supper, that is all. The family must have left a house servant and the gardener to guard their property while they are away.'

'So we can't go up into the house!' Mercy's eyes were big in the dim light. 'We have to stay in the dark!'

'We can be cosy down here,' whispered Nick. 'It's only for one night. I'll find us a better place tomorrow, a truly empty place, I promise.'

'Did the man up there hear us, do you think?' asked Mercy. 'Will he come with a stick and a dog, looking for …?'

'If he does hear us he'll think it's just rats in the cellar,' said Nick.

Mercy clutched at Nick's sleeve. 'Are there really rats?'

'No,' said Nick, but he knew that there probably were. Nick took off his jacket and wrapped it around Mercy. It was cool in the cellar, but he wrapped her more for the comfort of being wrapped tight like a baby in swaddling than for the warmth of it.

'Nick?'

'Yes.'

'Do you suppose that Mother is dead now?'

Nick paused. 'Yes, I think so,' he said. 'I hope so. She will be at peace and with Father now.' He held Mercy tight. 'We should pray for her soul. Then perhaps eat a little of the bread, and sleep.'

Mercy snuggled close. She looked up at Nick in the darkness, and he could see that her eyes were big. 'I can't bring Mother to mind, Nick. I can't remember what she looks like properly.'

'I'm the same,' admitted Nick in puzzlement. 'But I think we will remember her more clearly after today is over, perhaps.'

Mercy began to weep. 'Why did God make her die, Nick? Why?'

'Because he was angry,' said Nick, and he felt anger thrashing around inside himself too. 'Remember in the Bible? How God was angry, so he sent the flood to kill all the people except for Noah and his family? Well, it's like that again. God is angry with the King and his friends who live such sinful lives.'

'Then why is it that the King stays safe while everybody else is dying?'

'I don't know,' said Nick. 'But you and I, Mercy, we will be like Noah. We will keep alive.'

'I hope so,' said Mercy. She yawned.

'Bed,' said Nick.

'But we have no bed.'

'Aha,' said Nick. 'We do have a bed. It's just that you can't see it in the dark.' Mercy was familiar with this game and Nick could feel her relaxing against him.

'Go on,' said Mercy. 'Make it grand.'

'Very well,' said Nick. 'Now, let me see. Ah, yes. You, my Mistress Mercy, are wrapped in a silken coverlet embroidered with flowers and birds of all kinds.'

'Not ravens,' said Mercy. 'I don't like ravens.'

'Not ravens,' agreed Nick. 'But peacocks and swans and every beautiful kind of bird. You have just eaten syllabub ...' Mercy sat up.

'Don't talk about food,' she said. 'It will make me hungry for what I cannot have. Tell a story instead. Please?'

'Very well. Lie still, then.'

'Which story is it to be?'

'The Fat Hens and the Thin Hens.'

'I remember!'

'Shush!' Nick put a finger to Mercy's lips, and she lay still. 'Well, there was once a farmyard full of cows and sheep and …'

'Hens! There were hens!'

'There were a dozen hens, all penned together inside the farmyard just as we are penned within the walls of London.'

'That's not in the …'

'Shush! I'm telling this story, not you! Well, some of the hens were poor skinny things with knobbly knees and tatty black and brown feathers. They scratched for grubs in the soil and seeds from the grass all day long. But there were other hens in the yard, fat lucky hens who pushed the skinny hens aside and pecked at any of them who tried to get near the farmer's wife when she came out sprinkling corn on the ground. I think those fat hens probably had coloured feathers that stuck out like frilled pantaloons around their legs, as fancy as the King's. Those fat hens fed their fill on the corn and left only a few poor husks for the skinny hens to eat.'

'Poor skinny ones.'

'Yes, poor skinny ones because not only were they hungry, but the fat hen folk cackled and clucked and felt themselves to be very fine indeed until …'

'Go on!'

'… Until the farmer's wife decided to give her family a roasted chicken for lunch. She came into the yard and she looked around and she saw the fattest hen of them all, as fat as Mistress Robinson up at the Tower.'

'Nick! You must not say that!'

'And the farmer's wife saw another hen with a beak as big as the King's nose.'

'Nick!'

'And the farmer's wife took hold of their two necks and she swung them into the house where she had them hung, drawn and quartered, and I dare say stuffed with apricots and walnuts and cooked in time for the farmer's dinner. And what do you think the skinny hens did then?'

'They laughed!'

'They did. And, after that, the fat hens were frightened every time the farmer's wife opened her door in case they were the next ones to be chosen. They tried to hide behind the skinny ones, but it never worked because the thin hens were too thin for fat hens to hide behind.'

Mercy laughed. 'Tell another story!' she said, suddenly sitting up.

'I thought you were tired!'

'No. Tell another bird story, Nick. Please?'

'I'll tell a little story about a raven.'

'I don't like …' Mercy pulled a hand from her jacket wrapping and thumped Nick on the arm.

'But this is a good story about a thirsty raven,' said Nick.

'I'm thir…'

'Shush! One hot dusty day a raven wanted a drink. He could smell water somewhere nearby, so he went looking for it. He found a tall thin jug that was half full of lovely cool clear water. But when the raven tried to drink, his beak wasn't long enough to reach down to the water. What could he do?'

'Knock the jug over?'

'No, silly! That'd spill the water and it would all be lost! No. This was a clever raven. He hopped over to a place where he found a pebble. He picked the pebble up in his beak, then hopped back to the water jug and dropped the pebble into it.'

'Why?'

'You'll see. He hopped around and found another pebble, then another and another, and he dropped them all into the jug. And each time he dropped in a pebble the water in the jug rose higher until …'

'The raven could reach to drink it!'

'That's it.'

'I still don't like ravens,' said Mercy.

'Just go to sleep,' said Nick, suddenly too tired to humour her any longer. He laid Mercy as comfortably as he could on the rough cellar floor. He felt the shape of her and found her head and shuffled himself under it to make her a pillow of his lap. Then he stroked and stroked her hair to sooth her to sleep. Don't think of Mother, he told himself as he stroked Mercy's hair on and on. But thoughts of Mother came at him anyway, thoughts that made him feel faint and dizzy. Nick breathed deeply and tried to stop the sick feeling from rushing up inside him.

As Mercy slumped asleep, Nick got up, and he wobbled. Perhaps he was just weak from hunger? Nick reached for the food bundle and he pulled out a piece of the meat to chew. It tasted rank, aged fast by the hot weather, but Nick pinched his nose shut and made himself eat that meat anyhow. They couldn't afford to be fussy about what they ate now. They had no money or spare clothes and little food and no drink. How long could they last without those things? Nick kicked the floor. Father's death and now Mother's, all the fault of that man; the King.

Nick felt the air, dark as soil, all around him in this underground place, and he gasped for breath. Sit down, Nick told himself. Calm yourself. But as he bent down he put his weight onto his hand, and there was something soft and furry that moved under it. Nick gasped and snatched his hand away. It was a mouse, dead and warm, squashed under his hand. Nick picked the dead mouse up by its tail, then he scrabbled up, out of the cellar, and out into the fresher air of the moonlit garden, where he threw the dead mouse as far as he could.

The garden was a black and white and grey place in the moonlight. It was quiet. Nick breathed in the space and freshness of it. He stretched his arms wide and felt calmer. Glancing up at the house, he saw that there was no glimmering candle light behind any of the windows, not even at the windows of the servants' rooms at the top of the house. Anyone inside must be asleep by now. So for a while the garden was his.

Nick didn't go far from the cellar in case Mercy woke and found herself alone, but he wandered under the apple trees. He found a few bruised or maggoty apples that the gardener hadn't thought worth taking into the house. It was a little more food that they could take and eat. As Nick bent to pick up another apple, something big and raggedy and black suddenly flapped towards him.

'Kraack!'

Nick instinctively ducked with his hands up to protect his head. Then he saw what had flapped and made the noise. A raven had landed and was jumping over the grass in great galloping leaps.

'You again!' said Nick. 'Isn't it?' He looked closely at the bird. He was almost sure that he recognised the shiny tar-black feathers that tufted up on top of the bird's head. 'My button-thief devilish friend!' said Nick. He had forgotten the button in all that had happened. He patted his breeches pocket now and felt the button still safe inside. One small item that he and Mercy could sell or exchange for food. 'Have you come stealing once more? Do ravens eat apples?' asked Nick. Then he saw. The raven had his eye on something other than apples. Its gleaming eyes looked towards the place where the dead mouse lay on the grass. The raven looked at

Nick, head quizzically on one side.

'Go on, take it,' said Nick. 'I don't want it.' The bird swivelled his head to look behind, and Nick realised that two other ravens had also landed, also attracted by the mouse. They were big ravens, fully grown. 'Go on,' Nick encouraged his raven. 'Eat it quick before those others get it.' His raven took a step forward and swung its sharp-beaked head up, then down, like a man working a pick-axe. But a moment later the raven wobbled unsteadily.. 'What is it?' A feeling of horror was creeping down Nick's neck. The bird was staggering very like the way that Mother had staggered when the plague came in her, very like a man who has had overmuch ale to drink. Suddenly the bird fell down onto the grass, stone-stiff. 'Oh, no!' whispered Nick.

The raven lay quite still, with its black three-toed feet up in the air like miniature winter trees. It's been poisoned by the mouse, thought Nick. The two other ravens were watching. Now they shifted uneasily on the grass, then flapped wide their dark wings and rose up into the night sky and away. Quick as a blink, Nick's raven flipped over onto its feet and began to peck at the mouse again. Nick laughed out loud. 'You crafty devil! You are as good an actor as any of them at the playhouse!

I see your game, pretending to be poisoned to put those others off wanting the mouse!'

Nick watched his bird tearing at the pink mouse flesh, then strutting across the grass, coming close to Nick. 'You have no fear at all, do you, Devil?' A pigeon or sparrow or thrush would have fled as soon as they had pecked up any food to be had, but the raven seemed to enjoy sauntering around the garden, side by side with Nick. Until it had suddenly had enough of that and flapped up into the sky, flying eastwards and away. Towards the Tower, thought Nick. That's where the ravens like to fly at night. He'd seen them, hoards of them, all tumbling in the sky together in a kind of dance with the moon behind them over the pale White Tower.

It seemed lonely in the garden once the raven had gone, and Nick thought of Mercy on her own too, down in the cellar. To carry the apples he'd found, he made a scoop of his shirt in the way his mother had used to use her apron to hold things when she didn't have a basket handy. Nick crawled back down into the cellar that blinded him with its darkness. He felt his way and unloaded the apples carefully onto the floor. He hoped that they wouldn't attract more mice.

He pushed the apples further away, just in case. Then he felt gently for the warm curve of Mercy on the floor and he lay down, curled around her. I shall have to learn to do tricks like my friend Devil if I am to keep you safe and fed, Mercy, he thought.

Nick slept, but it was a sleep full of nightmares about his mother that woke him, trembling, while it was still dark.

Chapter Four

Nick woke, sweating and shaking. Which doesn't make sense, he thought. You shake when you are cold and sweat when you are hot, and you can't be both at once, can you? The first grey light of morning dimly revealed the inside of the cellar as it shone through the open door. Mercy was still hunched in exhausted sleep on the floor, but Nick sat up, and he felt the cellar spin around him. He got onto his knees, then pushed up onto shaky legs. The cellar floor reared up and hit him and he lay on its hard gritty surface and didn't know whether he was on the ceiling looking down or on the floor looking up. A thought struck him, sharp as a dagger; Mother had staggered and clutched and fallen when the plague first entered her. Is that what's happening to me now, thought Nick? Have I brought the plague with us? Nick's mind spun like a Catherine wheel. He suddenly heaved and was very sick into a corner of the cellar, then lay down on the gritty floor, clammy and shaking.

Mercy! he thought. What would happen to Mercy if he died? She would be alone with his corpse in this dark cellar. Then she would fall ill with plague too and ... No! He must go from Mercy; run now and take the danger away from her. But that would leave her alone! Mercy was stirring, and Nick's mind sharpened into a plan. He knew that he mustn't let Mercy know that he was ill. It would scare her too much. He must take her and just leave her somewhere safe, very soon, while he could still walk. Who could care for Mercy? Mistress Jenkins? Everything that Nick and Mercy owned was in Mistress Jenkins's house, but that house would be nailed shut by now. No. They must go to Seth Binder and his good wife Pegg.

'Mercy!' Nick was sharp because he must get her to move and he dare not touch her. 'Mercy, you are to get up at once and climb out of the cellar.'

'What's that smell? Where ..."

'Hurry!'

'Again?'

'Again, but for the last time, I promise.'

Mercy rubbed bleary eyes and got stiffly to her feet. 'Where are we going now?'

'To pay a visit to Master Binder.'

'Master Binder who you work for?'

'That's it. You know Mistress Binder who gave you a skirt that once belonged to their little girl that drowned? We will go and visit her and I dare say she might give us a bite of breakfast.'

Mercy got slowly to her feet. 'Can't we stay here awhile? My feet are sore.'

'No we can't,' said Nick. Now get up through that door. Keep low and run to the gate. I shall be just behind.'

'Bossy!' said Mercy, but she did it. Thank God for that, thought Nick.

Being sick had eased the pain in Nick's stomach, but it left him feeling dizzy. Mercy mustn't see how I am, thought Nick. Nor Seth or he won't let us into his house. Nick took a deep breath. All I must do is get Mercy to Seth's house, and then she will be safe.

Mercy held out a hand to Nick and looked pleadingly up at him. But Nick folded his arms.

'You're too old for holding hands!' he told her. 'Can you not walk a bit faster?' Nick felt horribly weak. Keep angry to keep strong, he told himself.

So he thought of the deaths that the King had brought upon the Truelove family – Father, then Mother, and now him. Nick bunched his fists tight. 'Move!' he told Mercy, and she glared back at him.

'I hate you, Nicholas Truelove!'

'Good,' said Nick. 'Now go faster.'

Mercy had tears streaking her dirty face and her bottom lip was quivering by the time they reached the small house where the Binders lived. Seth's door was already open to the early heat of the day. Nick could see inside to a table spread with a cloth. There was a jug and a loaf of bread and a pot with Michaelmas daisies in it. It all looked clean and there was a chair with a welcoming lap that Nick longed to slump into, but he must not. He must not appear tired or ill at all, not if he was going to persuade the Binders to care for Mercy. Nick steadied his breathing, then he knocked on the door.

'Master Binder?'

There were footsteps. Somebody was at home.

'Nick? And young Mercy, is it?' Seth was frowning. 'Your mother, Mistress Truelove, I heard …' Nick saw distress and alarm in the man's eyes and he could see that Seth didn't know what to do, but then Pegg came bustling to the door.

'Never mind what you heard or didn't hear, Seth Binder,' she told her husband. 'It's what you see with your own eyes that surely counts for more.'

Pegg Binder, pleasantly plump and carrying a pile of freshly washed linen, dumped the pile of linen into Seth's arms and came straight to Mercy. 'Gracious, man, can you not see that this little girl is in need of care? And just the same age as our Lucy when we lost her. How can you stand there idling?' Pegg put an arm around Mercy and scooped her into the house. 'Sit yourself down, my love, and I'll get you some of my barley water to drink. Your brother could do with some too, I dare say. Then you tell me what these tears are all about, eh?'

I should go now, thought Nick. Mercy is safe and I mustn't bring plague into the Binders' house or I will spoil it all. But Pegg was pouring barley water into pewter beakers and Nick's dry mouth felt like the dusty parched earth of the lanes outside.

'Here,' Pegg pressed a beaker into his hands as he stood awkwardly in the doorway. 'Come in and sit down and never mind Master Binder. You've come to see if Seth has more work for you, I dare say?'

'No,' said Nick. 'I thank you.' He tried to steady his shaking hands as they lifted the beaker and he drank, gulping down the cool liquid.

'My word, you do have a thirst!' said Pegg. She came at him, reaching out a hand to touch his hot forehead, but Seth gently took his wife's arm and steered her through a door and into the back room. 'Oh!' said Pegg. 'Excuse us a moment, would you?' The door closed, but Nick could hear a whispered argument between them. Seth was telling Pegg that it was too dangerous to take in children of a mother dead of the plague. But Pegg is kind, thought Nick. Surely she won't turn away Mercy, not if Mercy is on her own? I must go.

'Mercy?' whispered Nick.

'What is it?' Mercy wiped her face and scowled at Nick.

'I have a present for you.' Nick reached into his pocket and took out the silver button that the raven had given him only yesterday, though that seemed a distant time ago now. He threw the button carefully and Mercy instinctively put out her hands and caught it. She held the button between finger and thumb and tilted it in the light. Her eyes opened wide.

'It's silver,' said Nick. 'It is worth a deal of money.'

'Did you steal it?' whispered Mercy.

'No,' said Nick. It was given me by a friend. Now keep it safe and don't tell anybody of it. If you need to, you can sell it or exchange it. Do you understand?'

Mercy stroked a finger over the button and smiled for the first time that day. 'I know just the place to hide it,' she said. 'I'll sew it onto my bodice. That has a button missing.'

'Then everybody will see it, you goose!' said Nick.

'Goose yourself,' said Mercy. 'I'll cover it. I shall take a snippet of cloth from the hem of my skirt and wrap it around the button and nobody will know that it's special.'

Nick smiled. 'You're a clever girl, Mercy. And a good sister. And ...' There was the clatter of Seth lifting the latch on the door from the back room. Nick turned and ran, out of Shoe Lane, out of their sight. And out of Mercy's life.

Chapter Five

Nick stumbled over the cobbles, staggering in a kind of hot fog of fever that forced him to slump against a wall while the world spun around him like the blurred spokes of a carriage wheel. He gasped for breath and sense. It was done. Mercy was safe. But what about him? Was he to lie in the filth of the streets and alleyways until somebody noticed? Then be hounded and dragged to the stinking Pest House to die in the company of hundreds of people, all being tortured towards death by the plague? Nick pushed himself upright. He was too scared to stay still and be caught like that. Better to walk and walk while he could, walk until he dropped dead where he fell. Nick put hands under his armpits. No swelling. Just the fever that dizzied and drained him of strength.

By some instinct to head for open air, Nick found himself back at Tower Wharf by midday.

He tipped his aching head back and looked up at the Tower, as strong and sure as Nick was feeble. There were dark specs circling over the Tower that Nick thought to be a trick of his sick eyes, until her recognised them as ravens. One raven flew free of the others and came towards Nick, larger and closer until its wings spread wide and its feet braced in front of it to land at Nick's feet. Nick laughed, unsure whether this was dream or truth.

'Good morning, Sir Devil Raven,' he said. The bird pecked crossly at Nick's shoe, and the sharpness of his beak was real enough.

Nick pulled his foot away. 'I haven't any food for you this time, nor food for myself either.' Nick crouched down and wondered if he would ever be able to get up again. 'Do you know me?' It was the same bird, Nick was sure of it and he was strangely glad of its small gesture of companionship. The bird flapped his big wings, fanning Nick with a small breeze that cooled his fever for a moment. But when Nick opened his eyes, the bird was away, flying up and over the high walls into the Tower. The bird is a guest of His Majesty, thought Nick. Funny that a bird could come and go freely while men were taken into that place in chains to be locked up or killed. Nick laughed a little madly at the thought, and the laughing made his head throb so that the laugh turned into a groan. A woman passing by put a handkerchief to her mouth and hurried away from him. She sees I have the plague, thought Nick.

But through the hot hurting muddle of his mind there was suddenly an ice-cool clear idea that sliced through it all and made a sudden kind of sense. In his illness, Nick knew that he had a power that he could use for a wonderful revenge. If he could find a way to follow that raven into the Tower, then he could carry the plague into the domain of the King whose war-mongering had killed Father and whose wickedness had brought the wrath of God into London as plague and killed Mother. Those great stone walls were mighty defence against soldiers and guns and swords, but if Nick could take the plague inside those Tower walls, then justice might be done in bringing death to King Charles. Then God could rest from his anger with London, and London's plague would end. How beautifully logical and right, and exciting too! He, Nicholas Truelove, might kill the King and save London's people!

If only I could flap wings and rise up and fly over the walls as the raven does, thought Nick.

He couldn't fly, but maybe he could use a little of the raven's cunning? If he could only appear as ordinary and right in this place as one of those birds, then maybe he could appear invisible to the guards too? But how?

Pushing sweaty black hair from his face, Nick rested in the dark cool shadow of a wall and watched the Tower's guarded gateway. A group of men walked towards the gate. One of the men spoke to the soldiers, and the gates were opened and the soldiers stepped aside to let the men through. Then a grand gentleman with a boy attendant was saluted and they let him through without any hesitation. Following them came two carts rumbling over the cobbles. The men on guard stopped the first cart, lifting its cloth covering to inspect what was underneath, but they were just waving through the second cart, heaped with plump sacks. The sacks must have grain in them because there were pigeons fussing behind the cart, fighting to pick up whatever was dribbling from a hole in one of them just as seagulls will follow a farmer's plough to get the worms turned up in the fresh soil. With the guards distracted, Nick saw his chance. He hurried across to slip in amongst that flurry of birds and tag behind the cart. He put a hand on the back of one fat sack as if he was helping to steer it through the gateway.

Here, what are you after?' asked the carter, twisting around in his seat.

'Just shooing the birds from stealing your grain,' said Nick.

'Well, you'll get no payment from me for doing it,' said the carter.One soldier looked up at the commotion. Nick smiled across at him and shrugged. 'He's my uncle,' he said. 'Mean as anything!' The soldier grinned back, and Nick kept walking on and through the gateway, into the Tower. As the cart rumbled into what appeared to be the busy street of a small town, Nick took his hand from the cart and let it go ahead and away.

I've done it, thought Nick. I'm within the King's stronghold! He tried to stop his mouth from grinning in triumph. If only Mercy could know what he had done! Nick suddenly noticed a man scowling at him. Ducking down, Nick pretended to adjust his shoe lacing, then he straightened and set off at a feeble kind of a run, trying to look like a boy in a hurry, on some errand and too busy to be stopped. Don't look back, he told himself. Remember that the trick is to look the part of a boy who belongs in this place.

It took all his slight energy to keep running and keep upright. Panting feverish breath, his legs ready to buckle under him, Nick came to an open space where lines of soldiers with breastplates glinting in the sun stood smartly to attention in front of the White Tower. And, as Nick folded over, clutching his knees and fighting the swirling sickly dizziness that made the world seem to lurch around him, he laughed. Because there in front of the soldiers was his friend, the tuft-headed raven, once more, strutting up and down just as though he was the soldiers' commander. Am I seeing what isn't there because of my fever, wondered Nick? The bird's black wings crossed tips behind his back and his head tipped back to let his blackcurrant eyes inspect the soldiers' gleam.

'Kraack!' he told them in a firm voice, and Nick almost expected the soldiers to obey the command in some way, but …

'Got you, you young rogue!'

A cool shadow darkened over Nick and a hairy hand clamped tight to the scruff of his shirt, making him choke, turning him to face a big giant of a man, red-faced under a hot grey wig that wobbled with rage.

Chapter Six

'Let go!' gasped Nick.

'Are you a spy?' bellowed the man. 'Working for the French? Or the Dutch? Or those who are against the King within our own country?'

'No!' Nick struggled. But his fever seemed to have drained his strength, and his attempt to escape the man's grasp was so feeble that the big man laughed.

'Not a very great threat to His Majesty, I think!'

'Kraack!' The raven was suddenly flapping at the man's legs, threatening with his beak. And Nick remembered that he had a weapon of his own too. He was about to declare himself a carrier of the plague. The man would let him go quick enough if he knew that! But Nick thought how that would bring a quick end to his time in the Tower. He must be cleverer than that if he was to stay long enough to bring sickness near to the King. Nick tried to think clearly.

'You should let go of me,' he told the man, enjoying breathing disease up into his face. 'I am here on an important errand.'

'Indeed?' sneered the man. 'And what kind of errand would that be?'

'I have a message. For Sir John Robinson.'

'Oh, yes? And who is the message from?' The man let Nick go, but stood so close that Nick could smell the sourness of his sweat. 'A message from the King perhaps?' he asked, smiling at his own joke.

Nick tried to stand tall and firm. 'Indeed,' he said. 'It is a message for Sir John from the King.'

The man chortled. 'Oh, my! Well, in that case I had better not delay you any longer or I could be accused of treason, could I not? Give me the message and I will see that Sir John receives it.' The man held out a hand, then smiled when Nick shook his head.

'The message is not written down,' Nick told him. 'I am to tell it to Sir John in person.'

The man curled his lip. 'Then I had better hurry you straight to him!' He grabbed hold of the back of Nick's shirt and marched him up to and through a door into a grand white house. Inside smelled of wax polish and rich food and sweet wood fires.

Sunlight shone on polished furniture and rich colours on the floor and walls. Nick reached out to take hold of a chair to steady himself, but the man swiped his hand away, and Nick staggered.

'Stand up straight,' said the man. There was a sneer in his voice. 'Or some might not believe that you are truly on a mission for the King!' The man straightened his wig and brushed a hand to smooth his jacket front. 'Now then,' he said. 'Sir John and Lady Robinson are dining with guests at present, but I am sure that he will want to be interrupted by such urgent business.'

'It could wait awhile.' Nick cleared his throat and tried to sound braver. 'In fact, I think that the King would rather that I told Sir John the message without other company present.'

But the man had already burst through a great white door into a room full of colour and laughter and smells of spiced food that made Nick gasp for breath.

'Gracious, Bailey, whatever have you got there?'

Sir John slouched in a fine leather-padded chair pushed back from the table. His waistcoat was unbuttoned and his wig was slightly askew. Mister Bailey's hand prodded Nick's back to push him forward. 'It is a boy, Sir.'

'A boy?'

The five gentlemen, one large lady and a sulky looking boy stopped talking and all turned to look at Nick. Nick felt his ears go hot. Would Sir John recognise him from the incident on the wharf? Would they see the sickness in him and have him flogged for daring to bring disease into their home? Nick looked down at his ragged shoes on the fine Turkish rug. Mister Bailey jerked him upright again.

'This boy sneaked through the gates, Sir John. I followed and caught him.'

'Then deal with him, Bailey!' said Sir John. 'Why serve him up as if he were a plate of gilt gingerbread to finish off our meal? I don't find him in the least bit appetizing!' Sir John looked around the table, and the company all laughed a little at his joke.

Mister Bailey put a hand to his mouth and did a small cough. 'I thought to bring him straight to you, Sir John, because ...' Mister Bailey left a dramatic pause and tilted his head back. 'Because the boy tells me, Sir John, that he has come to us on an errand from the King.'

'From His Majesty?'

Now there was real laughter around the table.

Nick felt his heart thumping hard within his chest. He saw the boy roll his eyes at the large woman and pinch his nose. The boy had fair curling hair and clothes as fine and fancy as those worn by the older people present. Nick glanced down at his own sweat-filthy torn shirt. A shirt cut down by Mother from an old shirt of Father's. Yes, thought Nick as he looked at the boy, I probably do stink, but I don't look as stupid as you do in your lace frills! He stared hard at the boy, until the boy turned away and pretended to be busy slicing an orange.

'Well?' Sir John was wiping a napkin over his mouth. 'What does His Majesty want with me so urgently that he must send word with so unusual a messenger? Your message must be something of mighty importance. Something very secret perhaps? A matter of war, I shouldn't wonder. Are we to surrender to the Dutch and deliver them His Majesty's crown and sceptre? Or perhaps I am to let the lions loose from the Tower zoo to chase the last of the pestilence within the city walls?' Around the table, chins and wigs wobbled with laughter. The boy snorted a scornful laugh at Nick. Sir John was enjoying himself. He doesn't know me from the wharf, realised Nick. He felt the power in that. I know more about you, Sir John, than you know about me, he thought. And I am sick with the plague and have nothing to lose since I am bound to die soon anyway. I have the advantage here, for all that you have the money and position to scorn me.

Sir John went on, 'Maybe His Majesty wishes me to declare a public holiday and place wine in all the city fountains as we did for his coronation? With fireworks too, I wouldn't wonder. Well, boy? Has Mister Bailey understood you aright?'

Nick looked at the grand folk laughing at him. He felt the heat of indignation at the back of his neck. But, strangely, he was feeling stronger now, steadier. He remembered a child who had laughed at him years ago when he and his parents first came to the city. The boy had scorned Nick because Nick had never ridden in a coach. That boy's father was a coachman and so the boy often took a ride in one. One day Nick's Father had overheard the taunting and he told the boy that very soon a Master Orrow would be coming in a very fine coach to collect Nick and take him wherever he cared to go. The boy had muttered something and gone away. And Nick had turned to his father and asked, 'Who is Master Orrow?

Is he really bringing me a coach?' And Father had tapped the side of his nose and told him, 'Master Orrow is a fellow called Tom, Nick. And you know as well as I do that Tom Orrow never truly arrives!' Father laughed then, but it wasn't until some while later that Nick understood the joke.

Nick smiled to himself and stood up straight and tall. He told Sir John, 'Sir, your man has both understood and misunderstood me. My message is from a man named King. He is a Master Jo King, Sir. He sent me here to tell you a piece of wisdom. He says to tell you that to have a stitch or two of a tapestry is not to see the whole picture clear.'

There was a moment's pause as these words worked on wine-addled brains. Then Sir John and the rest of them sitting at the table began to laugh. Mister Bailey suddenly cuffed Nick's head hard, then took rough hold of one of Nick's arms and twisted it up his back to make Nick dance on his toes. Lady Robinson held up a hand.

'No, Mister Bailey! The boy has the wit to make you look foolish, but that is no reason to hurt him in that horrid way!'

'Let the boy go, Bailey,' ordered Sir John, and he thumped a fist onto the table, making wine jump in the glass goblets. 'Ha!' he laughed. 'The cheeky scoundrel has you there, eh, Bailey! Master Jo King.' Sir John turned to his wife. 'Did you follow the joke, my dear? And the message is that to see a part of a thing is not to see all of it. That's very true,' he nodded. 'Very true.'

'I understood this boy very well from the start,' said Lady Robinson, lowering her head but looking directly at Nick through her eye-lashes. I see that this is a poor sort of boy, but one with pride and a degree of bravery that makes me think that he perhaps has noble blood in him to some degree. Is that so? What is your name, boy?'

'Nicholas,' said Nick.

'Nicholas whom? The family name is the important part of it.'

Nick thought of the trouble that he intended to bring to these smug people and their master and he knew that the blame for such trouble must never come to land on Mercy. The name Truelove must be kept secret and he must find a different name for the character he was playing.

'Raven, my Lady,' said Nick. 'My name is Nicholas Raven.'

'Indeed?'

'Indeed,' said Nick, and he thought, that is truly who I am now. I am Master Raven, as cunning and quick as my bird friend. I shall use these people who serve the King as I want, and then I shall go to my death. But Nick saw and smelled the remains of food on the table in front of him, and it was hunger rather than sickness that he felt now. Well, he told himself, why not try your raven cunning and see if you can earn yourself a bite to eat? Play the servant in order to be the master. So Nick rubbed one dirty shoe down the back of his rumpled stocking. He let his head drop humbly. He looked at the table, at a pie with a pastry crust crumbling into rich brown gravy. He looked at the fruits spilling over the edge of a silver plate. He put his head on one side in the way that had endeared the raven to him enough to offer the bird a crumb.

Lady Robinson popped a sugared plum into her own mouth and then waved a hand towards Nick. 'The poor soul!' she said. 'There is hunger in his eyes. He is no older than you, James, do you see?'

The boy, James Robinson, curled his lip. 'Send him home to his dinner, then, Mother.'

'Does he have a home?' said Lady Robinson, her eyebrows arched. 'You do not come from a place with the pestilence within it, do you, Nicholas Raven?' She snatched a posy of herbs that sat beside her dinner plate and she put the posy to her nose.

'Madam,' assured Nick. 'I am from the country near the sea where the salt air has kept the disease well away.' That wasn't a lie. Nick and his parents had moved from the coast when he was small. And, after all, Nick had given fair warning that to know a little of something was not to see all of it.

Lady Robinson frowned. 'Then why come to London at this time when those any with sense are fleeing it? Why have you come to the Tower, Raven?'

'Why, My Lady Robinson,' Nick smiled at her. I want to serve my sovereign lord, our good King Charles. That is why I came to his Tower and to his truest friend, Sir John Robinson. I am here to offer my services.'

'Gracious!' said Lady Robinson. 'A noble aim expressed with enough grease to slip your way out of the trouble Mister Bailey hoped to trap you in. You are a bully, Mister Bailey! I suggest, Sir John, that we take this Nicholas Raven into our household.'

Sir John looked startled. 'Really? Take him on as what exactly, my dear? Should we lay him against the crack under the door to keep out the draught? The boy has no skill that we know of and, besides, he is far from clean.' Sir John wrinkled his nose.

Lady Robinson took another sugared plum from the plate. 'A good wash can put that to rights. As I say, my dear, he is much the same age as James, by the look of him. Why not let James have him for a foot boy?'

'Mother!' There was disgust in James Robinson's voice, but Lady Robinson ignored him. She lent close to Sir John, and Nick heard her mutter, 'It will do no harm if a little of this boy's sharpness of spirit comes to rub off on James. What do you say?'

Sir John patted his full stomach. 'I say, let this Nicholas Raven show us how well he wishes to serve his King by serving his King's friend's son well. Now, let us turn our attentions to some music and perhaps a little more wine. Come!'

The grand people rose rather stiffly to their feet and made their unsteady way towards a door in the far wall. Lady Robinson was the last to leave the table. She gave Nick a great wink and tossed him a sugared plum. 'See him cleaned and told his duties, Mister Bailey.' She looked sternly at Nick. 'You were brought for punishment and we have been kind. I expect that kindness to be rewarded.'

For the first time Nick felt a twinge of guilt at the thought of what he had brought within the great Tower's walls. Then he bit into the plum oozing sticky sweetness and thought only of the wonder of the taste of it, until Mister Bailey grabbed him by the shirt neck once more.

'Move!' he said.

Chapter Seven

Down in the kitchens Nick was scrubbed clean and dressed in cast-offs from Master James. The clothes were far grander than anything Nick had worn before but they were rather short in the sleeve and wide in the waist. Wearing another boy's clothes gave Nick even more of a feeling of playing a part rather than being his true self. Washing had cooled and refreshed him. And eating a piece of pie and drinking the small ale put in front of him by Cook made him feel stronger.

'Here, young Raven,' said Cook, handing Nick a cup of milk. This one isn't for you. You're to take it to Master James. You take it up to him, quick smart.'

'Which way?' asked Nick, and Cook told him how to find James's room.

So Nick set off up the polished stairs with the cup of milk. He could smell the good clean creaminess of it and his fever seemed to have left him with an endless thirst. Nick wondered what his raven friend would do if such temptation was offered him. Nick stopped at the top of the broad polished stairs. He glanced over his shoulder to check that nobody was watching. Then he lifted and tipped the cup to swallow a good swig of smooth milk. Wiping the back of a hand over his mouth, he grinned. There was a blue and white vase of late summer roses on a table beside him. Nick tipped a little water from the vase into what was left of the milk to top it up before he knocked on Master James's door.

'Come!' said James's haughty voice, and Nick pushed open the door.

James Robinson took the cup and drank. Then he wrinkled his face in disapproval.

'This milk tastes too thin,' he declared.

'Ah yes, it will do, Master James,' said Nick, head bowing a little as a good servant's should. 'They told me in the kitchen that the milkmaid who brought the milk this morning warned that today's milk was bound to come a little thin on account of there being so much dew in the night. The cows supped-in the water on the grass along with the grass itself. That is how it works, you know. Cows chew grass and work it into milk.'

'I know that very well! scowled James.

'Then you will understand that such thin milk cannot be helped when there is rain or a dew the night before a cow is milked.'

'I never heard that part of it before.'

'But I dare say that a fine gentleman like yourself has few dealings with cows,' said Nick, knocking fluff from James's jacket with a little more vigour than was necessary. 'It is something that is well known to us country folk.'

'Oh,' said James. Then he tipped his head back, nose lifted to compensate for his short height. 'Well, country folk should know a good deal about brushing dust off shoes and such. So see that the pile in the corner is cleaned and hung properly. Then you must tidy my room and clean my firearms before the tutor arrives. Do you hear that, Raven?'

'Yes, Sir,' said Nick, and he longed to trip Master James Robinson so that he might fall on that long nose of his and dent and bloody it.

As he moved through that first day, Nick began to suspect something. When night came and he lay on the small pallet in the kitchen of the grand house within the walls of the Tower, Nick was sure of it. He did not have the plague. His fever had left him. There were no swellings when he felt over his body. Even his headache had dulled so that it hardly bothered him now. He was tired, exhausted by all that had happened in the last two days, but he lay with his eyes open, uneasy. He felt adrift, unsure of both the world and himself. He felt stronger in his body, yet, strangely, that healthiness made him feel weak as well. Nick's eyes became hot and he knew that tears would fall if be blinked. His weapon had been taken from him. Without the plague he no longer had the power to harm the King. But you can live, he told himself! God has let you keep life, so use it! Go back and be a brother to Mercy! How could any sane person mind finding themselves to be well when they had thought themselves to be dying?

Nick turned on his side and curled tight. The tears came and took him over, shuddering him with sobs that clenched every muscle in his body until they hurt. Nick let himself think of Mother. He thought of Father. He turned onto his front and arched his back like an animal in pain and he thumped clenched fists onto the bed.

'Damned King! Bloody man!'

Surely there must still be some way to damage the King, even without the plague? Nick got up.

He went to the window where he leaned on the sill and looked up beyond the walls of the Tower to a sky salted with stars. If he could not harm the King himself, then maybe he could harm the Tower that held the King's power? Nick thought of the ancient White Tower, full of the King's weaponry. He crept back from the window and slipped under his cover, to sleep at last and dream of flying over the great White Tower.

Chapter Eight

As Nick helped James Robinson to dress the next morning, he asked James, 'Do you think a boy could ever fly?' As soon as he'd said it, Nick realised it wasn't the kind of question a servant should ask his master, but luckily it seemed to interest James. James walked over to the window and looked out.

'To fly would surely require wings,' he said. 'I wonder, could such things be made? Gracious, Raven, we shall have to experiment and see if it might be done!'

'Do you think, Sir, perhaps the birds can show us how?' asked Nick.

'But the stupid things are too far away to see properly,' complained James.

'Well, Sir,' said Nick, feeling bolder. 'I do know of one bird who might come near if we tempted him with a piece of something tasty. Meat is what a raven likes best.'

'Oh, very good!' scorned James, his nose suddenly tilted upwards. 'You cannot fool me with that one! You're talking about yourself, are you not? You are the 'raven' who would come close if I offered a good meat pie!'

'No, Sir,' assured Nick. 'This is a real bird that I know. He lives up on the wall of the White Tower.'

James waved a hand towards the window. 'There are scores of ravens. How can you tell one of the wretched things from another?'

'I have met it by the river, and in the lanes.'

'Where you lived?'

'Yes,' said Nick, then he saw the look on James's face and knew that he had told too much of the truth.

'So,' sneered James. 'You are not from the country as you told my mother. You have lived in the lanes after all, and with the plague around!'

'I have lately lived in the west of the city where there is little plague.' That was true. 'I was from the country before that,' said Nick. That was true too. James needn't know how many years went between the two.

'Well,' considered James. 'Show me this bird of yours and then help me to construct some wings, and I may forget to tell my parents what you have told me.'

'Then the first thing to do is to beg a little meat from Cook,' said Nick.

When Nick called, 'Kraack!' and waved a bit of raw meat at the base of the Tower wall, his raven flew down and then hopped across the courtyard towards the two boys.

'He is bigger than I had thought,' said James, taking a step back. But Nick crouched down and held out the meat and the raven's plumed head snatched and tore at it. James waved a hand, 'Pull open a wing so that we can see how it is structured,' he said.

'No,' said Nick.

'Why ever not?'

Nick didn't want to tell his real reason. The truth was that Devil came to him by choice and if Nick abused that friendship, he knew that the raven might never come close to him again.

James picked up a small stone and threw it at Devil. 'Open your wings, you stupid creature!' The stone missed and the bird didn't flinch but it gave James a withering look. Instantly Nick was on his feet and looking down at his young master.

'You just stay still, Sir!' He glared at James. 'I will ask the bird to fly. Nick turned to Devil. 'Go now!' he said. And Devil bloomed wide his wings, then hopped, hopped and was up into the air, seeming to shrink as it flew up into the sky.

'A structure somewhat like a fan,' observed James, too interested in the science of what he saw to bother with Nick's manners just then.

'That is just how it should be,' said Nick. 'But it will not be an easy thing to achieve.'

They tried to zig-zag some spoiled chart paper that James had been allowed to take from Sir John's office. They folded and turned and folded again until the paper would close down onto itself to make a slim pile that would open out like a wing. 'But it is far too small to hold us up,' said James. We should try a cloak. That would be the right sort of a shape. Fetch one.' But somebody else was ordering Nick too.

'Raven!' called Mister Bailey. 'Go to the gardener and fetch a fresh nosegay to my Lady Robinson as quick as can be. My lady is to go out visiting into the city and must be protected from the vapours. Quick, boy!'

When Nick got to Lady Robinson with the posy of herbs and flowers, she asked him, 'Whatever have you led my son into now? James came asking me just now for the loan of a fan. I hope that he is not thinking of dressing as a girl!'

'No, my lady,' assured Nick. 'He is interested in how it can be that birds fly.'

Lady Robinson looked sharply at Nick. 'You mean that you boys are making wings? You are not the first to try that, you know.' She bent plumply towards Nick so that her maid would not hear. 'You might find this hard to believe, young man, but I tried it once myself when I was a girl. I distinctly remember jumping off some steps with a sheet held aloft and flapping like a startled goose. I fell like a stone, of course, and ripped my skirts. Don't smirk, boy! I was not so ample in those days!" She gave Nick a mock cuff over the head. 'So,' she said as she pulled on gloves in spite of the heat of the day, 'I should look to see you taking off from the roof of the White Tower, should I?' She chuckled and wagged a finger at Nick. 'Just you remember that James is Sir John's son, and heir to the Robinson name, as well as being my own precious boy. Shield him from harm, Raven. Do you hear me?' She smiled, put the nosegay to her face and swept out of the room.

'Yes, my lady,' said Nick.

Nick ran back to James's room. 'Master James, Sir, I have another idea for you; one given to me by your mother. We must use sheets to make the wings. A sheet will be lighter than a cloak and much stronger and bigger than paper.'

James curled a lip. 'I have been thinking,' he said. 'It won't work. It can't work. If men could ever fly, then somebody would surely have done it already. They haven't, so clearly it cannot be done.'

'But we can't truly know that unless we try!' said Nick. Here was his chance to get inside the White Tower and to the seat of the King's power.

'It is simple,' said James. 'We cannot be birds and birds cannot be us. Fetch me a drink, Raven.'

Nick's hands clenched tight as he dared to say, 'Of course you are yourself a little like one kind of bird already, Master James.'

'Whatever do you mean?' James frowned.

Nick tucked his fists under his armpits and waggled his elbows. 'You are very like the chicken that has had its wings clipped so that it will never fly!' he said, and he made clucking sounds.

'How dare you!' James's face was red. 'I shall tell my father what you said! I'll ...'

Nick raised one eyebrow. 'Tell your mother what I said?' asked Nick. 'Tell her that you dare not jump from any small height and try to fly? Yet she told me herself that it is something that she did in her youth. Are you less of a man than your mother, Master James?'

James stuck his jaw out. 'How dare you!' He tilted back his head, nose pointing upwards. 'I shall jump,' he said. 'Just fetch a sheet and tell me where you would have me jump from and you shall see me do it.' There was a pause. Nick felt a chill of power and evil mixing in him.

'Then jump from the White Tower,' he said.

'Don't be ridiculous, Raven!'

Nick's face softened. 'Not to jump off the Tower, Master James. That would be madness. No. Just to try the sheet in the wind that will be stronger up on the roof there, that is all. It should act like a sail on one of His Majesty's yachts, holding the wind to let the force of that wind power it along. We could feel that power transferred to our arms rather than a boat and try to work out a way to use it for flight. You are not too chicken for that small experiment, surely?'

James shook his head.

'Excellent,' said Nick. 'Then I shall go and fetch the sheet from off your bed, Sir.'

'At once, please, Raven!'

Chapter Nine

Short plump James led the way to the White Tower. Tall dark skinny Nick hurried behind, carrying the bundle of sheet across the hot open space between the house and the Tower. Nick had a tight feeling in his throat now that they were about to enter the White Tower. He had no plan what to do when he got inside. I will see what is there and what can be done, he thought. Will they let two boys into such a place? But the soldiers guarding the Tower nodded respectfully to James Robinson, the son of their Lord Lieutenant. They stood aside to let the boys through the door.

Nick stepped into the cool inside of the stone building and he followed James up spiral stairs, up and up past men busy cleaning muskets; men who looked up, but never questioned or stopped the boys. Nick lingered and looked around and saw other guns and swords and pikes stacked, but what could he do to those? Snatch one and be jumped upon and arrested and no harm at all done to the King? If only I could get near to his jewels, he thought. Then I could take the crown that marks the man as the King anointed by God. What would God think of such an action?

'Hurry up, Raven!'

James was puffing as he climbed the stairs, around and up, floor after floor. Nick passed James and led the way upwards, suddenly eager to get out onto the high open rooftop. He stepped onto the griddle heat of the flat lead roof high above London, where a warm breeze gently buffeted over the low parapet walls. Nick's quest for a wind to fly sheet wings and his hunger for the King's jewels were suddenly forgotten as he stood still in the slightly salty air that blew from the east. He put down the sheet and leaned over the parapet.

'Look at that!' He turned to James. 'It is as though I'm looking down on one of your father's maps, except that this map lives and moves. See that carriage moving along Tower Street? And that man on horseback? They have no idea that they are being watched!'

Nick walked to look over all four sides of the Tower, looking down on the river, the boats, the dockyards, and on to the fields and villages and a distant glimmer of sun on the sea. He felt himself to be suddenly grown big and strong because the world seemed to have shrunk below his feet. Beside him, James too seemed to have forgotten what they had come up here for.

'You know, Raven,' said James, 'This tower was built with blood mixed into its mortar to make it most particularly strong. It has been fortress and home to every king of this land for hundreds and hundreds of years. Old Nolly Cromwell took it for his mob, of course, but ...'

'I wish Mercy could see this,' said Nick as he looked beyond London to the green countryside. He would like to take Mercy to that open country place of clean air and no plague. I would take her away from London and never return, he thought.

'Mercy? Who is Mercy for goodness' sake?' asked James.

'She is my sister,' said Nick. 'She was very cross when I saw her last.' Nick pointed between the stone uprights of the parapet towards the messy mass of the city. 'She is living over there,' he said. 'With a friend.'

'Why not with your parents?' asked James. But

Nick didn't want to reveal more, and fortunately James saw something else to interest him. 'Look at them!' he laughed. 'They have a deal to learn about marching!'

Nick looked down and saw something that brought the blood hammering hot inside his head once more. A line of pressed men were being pushed and bullied towards the parade ground by soldiers. Men in chains, shuffling in fear, just as Father must have done. Nick's fists clenched tight, but James was already bored with laughing at the men and was back onto the subject of Mercy.

'If we can see where your sister is, then surely she could also see us,' he said.

'She doesn't know that I am here,' muttered Nick. 'This is the last place she would think to see me.'

'Then we should signal to her,' said James. 'Signal as the navy ships signal to each other, with flags.'

'Flags?' said Nick, suddenly paying attention. He looked at the pale sheet crumpled on the roof and thought of seeing that sheet flying boldly from the roof of the White Tower for all of London to see. A white flag: a message of surrender. Here, suddenly, was a chance to truly damage the King!

Surrendering to the Dutch would bring an end to the war, an end to the need to press men into service in the King's navy, an end to at least one kind of killing that the King inflicted on his people. 'Go on then, Master James,' said Nick. 'Hoist the sheet aloft and let it wave in the wind to my sister.'

James took two corners of the sheet and he lifted his arms and flapped the thing as a washerwoman would, but with less skill.

'Nobody will see that!' scoffed Nick. 'It isn't high enough to be seen above the parapet!'

James turned a darker pink. 'Then perhaps you would like to show how it could be raised higher, Nicholas Raven? Since you are such friends with the birds. Or maybe it is you who are the chicken after all?' James thrust the sheet into Nick's hands. 'Climb that turret and tie the sheet to the pinnacle, I tell you. Or don't you dare?' James tilted his head back and sneeringly stared at Nick. He pointed to the salt-pot-shaped corner turret made of stone topped with a lead cap and a pinnacle. 'You are my servant, Raven, and I order you to do it.'

And suddenly it made perfect sense to Nick to do exactly that. He flapped open the sheet and put a corner of it between his teeth to leave his hands free as he stepped up onto the parapet and reached for the stonework of the turret. He hugged around the hard corner of the turret's wall, clinging like a baby monkey to its mother, and he began to inch upwards and away from the foothold of the parapet.

Nick's mouth was dry from the sheet soaking up his spittle. He felt the cool strength of the stone that he clung to. He felt the empty nothingness of the air all around. And he looked up at the sheer stone wall to the blue sky beyond. The metal pinnacle was out of sight now, but Nick knew it was there, if only he could cling on and go upwards all that way. There was nothing to hold onto apart from the corner of the wall itself and it took every bit of Nick's concentration to clasp tight hold of the hard smooth stone. Almost instantly his legs began shaking weakly, feverishly.

'Kraack?'

A tatty black shape was silhouetted against the sun as Devil landed to perch on the roof cap above Nick, like a dark angel. Help me, Devil, thought Nick desperately.

'Come down, you fool!' called James from below.

Nick clasped the stone walls with his knees,

pushing upwards and reaching for a new hand-hold. But there was nothing for a hand to hold on to now. A strange slow cool calmness poured through Nick like chilled cream. He felt himself detaching from his own body, looking down on the dark boy perched perilously high, with a white sheet billowing like material breath from his mouth. If I am looking down on myself, then am I rising, wondered Nick? On my way to Heaven to be with Mother and Father? Then another thought hit him like a mallet. Mercy, still down there in the plague-ridden streets and with no family left at all if Nick were to go. Instantly, Nick plunged back into the body whose finger tips were screaming with the pain of holding onto smooth stone, his legs straining with the agony of it. Then the breeze suddenly tugged at the sheet, flapping it, pulling Nick over and away from the stone.

'Kraack!'

'Oh, do take care, Raven!' called James. 'Get down, I tell you!'

Nick's grasping fingers touched nothing at all now and he was tipping out over the long drop and he knew very well that he could not fly. But James's hand grabbed hard at his arm and tumbled him the other way, to land crashing, hurting, but safe onto the wonderfully solid hot lead roof.

'Good Lord, Raven,' said James as he looked down on Nick. 'You do realise that you very nearly died just then?'

'Yes, thank you, Sir,' whispered Nick.

Chapter Ten

'Whatever in the name of all the saints, and all the sinners too, by God, did you boys think that you were doing?' Sir John was red as a hot coal, stamping and hurrumphing as he paced up and down the council chamber in front of James and Nick. 'You have no more sense than this poker here!' Sir John picked up the long metal poker and brandished it like a sword. Nick and James both flinched. 'Far less sense than the fire iron, in fact, because a poker does no harm at all unless it is wielded by some person.' Sir John shook his wattled chins as a turkey might. 'And, by God, I feel like wielding it now on you two boys, I truly do!'

James stood, head bowed. Nick stared straight ahead.

'Do not look so sure of yourself, Raven. I care no more for the danger that you choose to put yourself in than I care what might happen to

Cook's cat. But I DO care for this country and for my King and, and for my own position and that of my family. Do you hear? Do you have any understanding of what you have done, I wonder? Here we stand in His Majesty's own fortress, in a state of war. Our ships are at sea, our countrymen fighting for us. You have surely heard the guns yourselves, for goodness' sake! And yet you attempt to raise a white flag from the topmost point on His Majesty's Tower?' Sir John raised his hands into the air in disbelief. 'My own son!'

'Sir John …' began Nick.

Sir John Robinson wheeled around and almost spat in Nick's face. 'No, Sir! I will not take any 'Sir John' and clever words from you.' He grabbed Nick by his shirt and lifted him up onto his toes. 'Oh, I know exactly whose idea this must have been. And I know exactly what I must do with you, you TRAITOR!'

'But Father …' said James, stepping forward.

'No, James.' Sir John was shaking his bewigged head. 'There can be no excusing this. None whatsoever. An attempt to send a signal of surrender? It is no more and no less than working for the enemy. It is treason.' Sir John pointed a plump finger at Nick. 'I should have you hung, drawn and quartered, boy. I should have your head spiked and on show for all to see!' Nick felt as if his insides had suddenly slid down below his knees, leaving the shell of him so weak and empty that he thought that he might crumple and fall. Sir John watched Nick's face, and he softened a little. 'You will be spared the hanging, Raven, but for one reason only. I want nobody, nobody at all or ever, to hear of what happened here today. Do you hear? Both of you? Above all else, the King must never, never know of it. Fortunately for us all it seems that your only observer was James's mother, travelling home and happening to look up from the coach. She, of course, will tell no-one. And neither will you, Raven, because you are going far away. I hope that you are fond of sugar? Well, now you can discover the joys of growing the stuff as well as eating it. I shall have you chained and sent to Barbados by the next boat.'

Nick felt sick, but now James was talking.

'You have it wrong, Father. It was I who ordered Raven to climb the turret with the sheet. As my servant, he naturally obeyed. So I am the one you should send to Barbados.' James smiled. 'Besides, I think I might like it there!'

'Don't be ridiculous, boy! Why are you telling me this?'

'Because, Father, you told me that I must always tell the truth. Well, if you send Raven to Barbados, I shall tell the truth. I may even tell the King what happened on the top of his Tower.'

'You would not!'

Nick thought that Sir John might burst open like a plum that has been stewed too long.

'I would, Sir,' declared James. And, to Nick's surprise, Sir John began to laugh.

'Do you know, I do believe that you would, you scoundrel! You always were an honest fellow, James, and it seems that perhaps you are a braver one than I gave you credit for. I'm not sure that I believe that Raven is entirely innocent. Still, I like to see loyalty as much as His Majesty does.' He looked at the boys sharply. 'Can I trust the two of you to tell nobody what happened up there today?'

'You can, said James, and Nick bowed ascent. Sir John looked to Nick.

'It seems that your young master values you. You may stay for the present.' He raised a finger. 'But you will work in the kitchen now, and I shall instruct Cook to work you hard. And if you bring any further trouble on my family …'

'I understand, Sir,' said Nick. Then he looked Sir John straight in the eye. 'And Master James, Sir. Master James is a fine bird, very unlike a chicken. More of an eagle, perhaps.'

'What the deuce are you blethering about now?' But Sir John saw a slow smile spread over his son's face. He chuckled and reached for a glass of wine from the table. 'You young people! Good Lord, Nicholas Raven, you have come to me for punishment and found reprieve yet again. I declare you have the luck of the very devil, do you not?'

Chapter Eleven

Next morning, the kitchen certainly felt like the devil's kitchen to Nick. The sweltering heat of late summer added to the steaming heat of boiling pans, the great fires and smoking fat to make it all so hot that there didn't feel to Nick to be any refreshment left in the air. He thought longingly of the breeze up on the Tower roof, and cursed himself for failing to hurt the King when he had the chance. He felt foolish. What now? Sir John no longer trusted him. Mercy hated him. Nick pushed lank hair off his sweaty brow and tore feathers from the poor dead duck on his lap.

'Gently, boy!' scolded Cook. 'It won't eat sweetly if it's been dealt with harshly. What's the matter with you?'

'Couldn't I go outside, just for a while? Fetch water or somesuch thing?' pleaded Nick. He felt pressed on all sides by the heat and smells of the place.

'Take a sup of this,' suggested Cook, and she passed him a cup of weak beer that was almost as warm as the kitchen. You're not going anywhere. Sir John said that you were not to. But I can tell you something that might cheer you, even though it means more work for us all.'

'What's that?' asked Nick.

'Well,' said Cook, rolling up her sleeves, ready to plunge her hands into a bowl of flour and spices. 'We are to have a visitor tomorrow. And who do you think that might be?'

Nick shrugged. He wasn't much interested.

''Tis only His Majesty!' grinned Cook.

'The King! Here?' Nick yanked hard at the feathers and muttered, 'I should dearly like to meet the King.'

Cook laughed. 'The nearest you'll get to that, my lad, is in meeting the dirty plates His Majesty has dined off!'

They kept cooking and cleaning and preparing well into the taper-lit darkness of that night, getting everything ready for the next day. There was hardly a moment to rest before the sun was up and the kitchen work resumed. A Frenchman was brought in to make a gilt and marzipan model of the King's barge to sit in the centre of the table and look grand. Cook was busy with pastries and pies. Butchers brought great sides of meat and a mass of birds of all shapes and sizes, and all needed preparing for the King's pleasure.

Nick's hands were busy peeling and plucking, but his mind was flying free and excited. Here was another chance to touch the King's life. Could he perhaps poison the King's food? A maid had just dropped and smashed a glass bottle of oil and Nick remembered hearing somewhere that crushed glass in food could kill a man. He bent to help pick up and pocket a piece of the sharp glass. But the more he thought of it, the less he liked the idea. What if another person ate or drank the poison instead of the King? He somehow cared about Sir John and Lady and James Robinson in spite of himself. Nick frowned. Even if he did manage to kill only the King, the scandal of the killing would fall upon the Robinsons. Nick pounded at the spices in the pestle, pounding his plan to nothing.

Nick suddenly longed to escape from it all, to forget about the King. He thought back to that moment on the Tower roof. He thought of the view he'd seen beyond London. And a new plan began to grow in his mind as the peppercorns turned to powder under his mortar. I'll take Mercy and together we'll get away from London and start a new life in the countryside, he thought.

'Raven?' Mister Bailey was suddenly beside Nick, and shouting. 'Did you hear me? Go and clean yourself. Master James has talked his father into letting him have you serve him today. Although why he needs ...' But Nick was already on his way out of that stifling kitchen and heading for the well's welcome cool water and the outside air.

As Nick lifted the bucket of water and poured it over his head, something big and black landed at his feet, attracted by the sunlight silvering and glinting on the running water.

'Devil?' said Nick. 'You won't be the only devil in this place today, you know. The King devil himself is coming to inspect the place and visit Sir John!'

'Kraack!'

'I don't doubt that His Majesty will take a glance at his fine jewels while he's here. Could you maybe pluck one from his hand for me, Devil? I'd give a fine titbit in return for a ruby or a pearl, or perhaps a big fat diamond!' Nick flicked water towards the raven and, head on one side, Devil pecked at the shining liquid, then raised his head to let it shower down his back. Nick tipped the last of the bucketful slowly, trickling it over the raven, and said, 'Why don't you leave London, Devil? I would have long ago if I was a bird and walls were nothing to me and food could be found any place. Or if I was a King and I could do just as I pleased.' Devil turned his back on Nick and lifted his tail high to expose a feathery bottom. Nick laughed. 'Ay,' he said. 'That's what I think of His Majesty too!'

'Raven?' Mister Bailey was shouting for him again. Nick put the bucket down and briefly touched Devil's head in farewell. 'You watch me today and see. I shall not bend my knee to King Charles even if he comes as close to me as I am to you. And I shall steal a piece of his feast for you, I promise!'

Chapter Twelve

Nick tugged the sleeves of the new dark green jacket over James's flounced cuffs. Then he stood back to see the overall effect.

'There,' said Nick. 'All is done and looks well.' It was something that Mother used to say when she had cleaned their room.

James scowled. 'I'd sooner be in shirt sleeves in this heat.'

'The coat is a very fine one if you are fond of flowers and ribbons,' said Nick. 'I suppose that if you want to please the King you must learn to follow His Majesty's taste in clothes instead of your own.'

James turned. 'Are you mocking me, Raven?'

'Not at all,' said Nick. 'I know very well what it is like, not being your own master. There are more kinds of servants here in London than some people realise.'

'Are you calling me a servant?' James could go

almost as pink as his father did.

'I'm saying that you and your father serve your King. By flattering his taste. I was making a compliment, Master James,' assured Nick.

'Oh.' James lowered his nose. 'Would you care to come and flatter the King yourself? Come down to the quayside with me. Father won't mind.'

So Nick stood in the sunshine behind Master James and Sir John and his lady and a gathering of important men and several servants as they waited for the King and his people to arrive. Nick felt much as a roasting joint must feel as he stood in his woollen jacket, hot and awkward. But then he looked towards the river and forgot all about heat and itchiness as he spotted the King's barge coming under London Bridge on its way from Whitehall.

'There!' James had seen it too. 'Look, Father!'

'Don't point!' scolded Sir John, but Lady Robinson put a hand on her husband's arm.

'Let him be, my dear. There's no harm in honest pleasure at the sight of His Majesty.'

Nick knew that he should not take pleasure from the sight of that evil man, but he couldn't look away, and a swell of cheering rose from the people all around him. Nick had seen the golden barge with its scarlet tasselled drapery on the river before, but only at a distance. Now, as the oarsmen raised their slim oars straight up like an avenue of young trees and the boat slid silkily through the water to nestle gently against the landing stage, Nick was dazzled by the rich beauty of the golden carvings. And he wasn't the only one to be attracted by the shine of it all in the sunlight. With clumsy flapping and a loud vulgar 'Kraack!', Devil flew down and landed on the quay, just where the King was about to step.

'Good Lord!' said Sir John, and he pulled a scented lace handkerchief from his sleeve and flapped it at the bird. 'Shoo! Shoo, you rude creature!'

But the raven stood solidly where he was. He put his head on one side and watched as a great tall ornament of a man stepped from the barge with five small yappy dogs excitedly tugging at the ends of ribbons all around him. The raven stood still, wing arms folded casually behind his back, and he looked at the dogs, unblinking. Sir John nudged the bird with a foot, but the raven didn't move.

'Kraack!'

'Go away!' Sir John looked desperately over his

shoulder and saw Nick laughing. 'You, Raven! Do something!'

So Nick crouched down and took the chunk of broken glass from his pocket. He turned it to make it glint in the sunlight. 'Here, friend,' he said, and the raven hopped in great clumsy jumps over to Nick. Nick threw the piece of glass into the air. 'Now go!' The raven reached out his wide black wings and beat up into the air above the heads of all.

'I see that you have your own bird boy, Robinson!' laughed the King. 'I had no idea you were fond of birds!' The King nodded to one of his men and the man held out a coin to Nick. It was gold.

'Thank you, Your Majesty,' said Nick, and he looked up into the King's face that looked down on him. The King was a taller man than any Nick had met before. He had big brown eyes above a large nose and thick lips roofed by a thin black moustache. Nick was beginning to bow in polite thanks when he remembered that this was the King who had killed his parents and put his sister into danger. Nick straightened stiff and scowled and didn't bow. The King and his retinue moved on. Nick clenched the coin tight. Money from the King. Enough to help him and Mercy escape from London, enough to start them on a new life! There was a little taste of justice in that, and Nick felt the satisfaction of it. And he hadn't bowed, not quite. He had kept his promise to Devil.

But Sir John Robinson kept bowing low, like a chicken pecking for corn, as he ushered the King and the other guests towards the Tower. The King's yapping dogs twirled around his stockinged legs, criss-crossing him with their ribbon leads so that the King began to resemble a maypole. His long black, curled wig flapped as he tried to disentangle himself. Nick smiled. The King glanced across at him and Nick stared boldly back.

'Take the damn dogs, would you?' said the King.

So Nick did, and he enjoyed the feeling of envy that came from James who had had no attention at all from the King.

But soon Nick was left alone with the dogs as the great men and the King went to do the King's business around the Tower. Nick could tell that there were matters at the Tower that displeased the King. The group of great men, and James with them, went into the White Tower and then across to the house, talking, talking. The King was shouting a little and Sir John kept on bowing, bowing as they went. It seemed to be talk of soldiers and armaments and money. But Nick was left in the yard with the ribbons and dogs. Mister Bailey brought bowls of fresh water and cuts of meat for the dogs, but he brought nothing for Nick. As the sun rose high in the sky, the dogs crowded into the small patch of shade by a wall and lay there panting small pink tongues. Time passed and the patch of shade shrunk smaller until the sun was right overhead. Nick scrunched his eyes against the glare of it. High on the Tower wall he could see Devil also watching the comings and goings. The heat made the air quiver above the hot stone paving like water. A fly buzzed. Nick could hear odd sounds of raised voices from inside the house. Devil flew down and paraded amongst the little dogs, eyeing the bright bells that hung from their collars and darting his beak at those bells. Devil stirred the dogs into a yapping tangle.

'Leave them be,' warned Nick crossly. 'You will have me in trouble with Mister Bailey.' He was trying to disentangle them all when suddenly the front door of the house opened and the King came striding out. He came straight over to Nick, the important men scurrying behind. Behind them came Sir John with his hands held out as if he was begging. 'But, Your Majesty, we have a dinner prepared. You must surely stay and dine. My Lady Robinson is awaiting us.'

The King turned and looked down at his Lord Lieutenant. 'And is it for you to tell the king what he surely must or mustn't do, eh, Sir John?' Sir John Robinson seemed to wither like paper in a flame. 'Is it your place to order me?' demanded the King, pushing his face close to Sir John's.

King Charles is a bully, thought Nick, surprised at finding himself indignant on Sir John's behalf. Nick felt an urge to put out a foot and trip that tall arrogant man in his silly ribbons and curls. But at that moment Devil spotted the glinting buckles on the King's shiny shoes and he lunged for them.

'Damn you, wretched bird!' The King was hopping and kicking and trying to get away from Devil's pick-axe beak, but the beak was following and stabbing at the silken royal ankles. 'Ow!' The dogs were yelping and spinning in hysterical circles, doing nothing to scare Devil away, but adding to the riot of it all. Nick laughed, and the King looked at him and narrowed his eyes. Nick stopped laughing. The King turned to Sir John.

'Get rid of that bird, Robinson! Him and all the others like him. There will be no ravens at my Tower by the time I next visit. Have them killed. Understand?'

'Certainly, Your Majesty,' bowed Sir John. And the King, his stocking torn and his shin bleeding, swirled his fine jacket and headed back to his barge with a flurry of followers and dogs behind him.

Nick felt hollow. Devil to be killed! All the ravens to be killed, on the King's orders. Would they be shot? Or poisoned? Why was it that London and the King always contrived to kill anything that Nick loved? The glory of the day shrivelled within Nick, and he was struck with the sudden thought that maybe even now Mercy was being destroyed too. Mister Bailey had said that the numbers dying of the plague were rising once again. Might it have found its way inside the Binder's home? Nick felt for the gold coin in his pocket. I'll go to her now, he thought. Show her this wealth and take her to safety away from London and the King.

Chapter Thirteen

'Go to the kitchen and help them with the meal,' Lady Robinson told Nick. 'The King may have gone, but we have other guests who are hungry and the food is all prepared. Take off that good jacket so that it isn't spoiled, then go and do as Cook asks. James, you may eat with us.'

'Can I take the King's place at table?' asked James.

'Certainly not,' said Lady Robinson. 'Bailey can bring a stool to be placed at the corner of the table for you. The King's chair shall remain empty.' With a rustle of skirts, she went. James grinned at Nick, then turned to follow his mother. He didn't hear Nick's muttered, 'Goodbye, Master James.'

They'll have to serve the meal without me, decided Nick. I'm going now, to Mercy. Nick hurried down to the kitchen, as he had been ordered to do. It was easy enough to tell Cook that he was on an errand for Lady Robinson, easy to slip between the very many people and very many dishes crammed into the hot kitchen and to knock a piece of sugar from the tall loaf of sugar on a shelf and put it into his pocket. He took a pinch of roast lamb too; a present for Devil. Nick bit his lip. Devil. Would Devil, with his uncanny intelligence, know somehow that he had been condemned to die? Might he have the sense to do as Nick was doing, and simply leave this place of danger? Nick hurried out of the kitchen, out of the house and back into the open afternoon air. He looked up and there were the ravens so high in the sky overhead that no harm could reach them just then. Nick put a hand to his brow to shade his eyes. 'Devil?'

'You want to look down, not up, if you're summoning the devil, lad!' laughed a soldier passing by. 'Is this heat getting to you?'

Nick shook his head, and he turned to go. He must leave quickly if he wasn't to attract notice and lose his own chance of escape. Nick threw down the meat, wiped his greasy fingers on his breeches, and hurried away. He mumbled a prayer for Devil's safety as he went. That was all he could think to do to help the bird, and he knew that it was feeble. He had prayed strongly enough for

Father and, more briefly, for Mother, yet neither of them had been spared. Was God more likely to come to the aid of a bird named Devil than for them? Nick felt torn between the needs of Devil and his sister, but Mercy was the more vulnerable of the two.

'On an errand for Sir John,' said Nick to the soldiers guarding the Tower gates, and he was allowed to walk out and down into the stench and shadows of the lanes and alleyways of London.

Cramped together and leaning over their narrow lanes, London's houses cut out the light and seemed to press around Nick in a way that he hadn't noticed when he lived amongst them. He turned along the familiar streets and lanes, seeing the places as an outsider might see them, noting how small and cramped and filthy things were. And there were dried and flaking blood-red crosses on some of the doors, and words that included his sister's name. 'God have Mercy,' they said. Nick began to run. The weight of the gold coin banging against his thigh felt reassuring. Could safety be found with such small wealth? Nick jogged along, dodging the beggars and the sealed doors and the worst of the piles of rubbish festering in the hot tunnel lanes. It seemed that

London had got sicker, even in the short time that he had been away from it. Would the Binders' door be marked too? Nick felt ill at the thought of it. He wished that he had a sweet-scented handkerchief of the kind that Lady Robinson was forever pressing to her nose or forehead. He felt faint with the heat and fright of it all by the time he got to the Binders' home and found that the door was mercifully bare.

'Thank God!' breathed Nick, and he pushed straight through to find Mercy standing at the table, mixing something in a bowl. She looked up as Nick barged into the room.

'Nick?' She didn't sound sure and Nick suddenly realised that he must look strange to her, dressed as he was in the fine clothes given to him by the Robinsons.

'Of course it's me, you goose!' he smiled, relieved to see her looking strong and fresh in a clean dress that moved in the breeze from the door. She had a new cap over her hair and tied under her chin; a red one. Made by Pegg, thought Nick, and he felt jealous on his mother's behalf. Nick held out his arms, wanting Mercy to come and hug him in her usual way, but she held back. 'I've come to take you back, Mercy,' he said. 'I've got money that will let us leave London.' Mercy just stared at him. Pegg Binder stepped quietly through from the back room. She came behind Mercy and stood there, a hand on the girl's shoulder. 'Good afternoon, Nicholas. Leave London and go where, do you suppose?' she asked gently, but with a firm look in her eye.

'To the country, to a place where we can be safe,' said Nick. He waved a hand at Mercy. 'Go and fetch your things, and we can go now.'

Mercy didn't move from the table. She reached out to take hold of one of Pegg's comfortable hands.

'We'd best go now,' said Nick, trying to sound firm, but his voice wavered. 'While we have some of the day still in front of us.' Mercy didn't move. 'Do as I tell you, Mercy!' said Nick.

'No!'

'No?'

'No, I shall not go with you!'

Nick felt as if he had been punched. He lifted his arms and stepped towards his sister. 'Why do you say such a thing? You must come! Do you not understand? It's to keep you safe. Besides, I'm your brother and you must do as I say!'

'No!'

'I have money. Look! It was given me by the King!'

Pegg had moved around the table to put herself between Mercy and Nick. She reached out a hand to touch Nick. He shrugged it away, but she put it back and pushed him towards a stool. 'Sit yourself down,' she said. 'Let us all calm down and share some small refreshment and talk with a bit of sense, eh?' As she took cups off a shelf and poured from a jug, she asked gently, 'And where exactly would you be taking your sister, Nick?'

'To the country. Out of London and away from the plague and the King and his evil people who do all they can to kill our sort and ...'

'You do know that you must have a Bill of Health before they will let you through the gates and out of the city?' said Pegg. 'And it takes the right sort of friends and lawyers as well as the right sort of money to get one of those. Besides, they aren't welcoming people into the country, I hear. The country people are all afraid that London people bring the plague along with them. There have been terrible things done to those who leave and try to settle in a new place. Do you have any family that you could go to out there, Nick? People to care for you?'

'I can care for Mercy myself,' said Nick, and Mercy glared at him across the table.

'I don't want you to care for me!' she said, her hands bunched into fists. 'I don't want to go to a strange place with strange people …'

'I'm no stranger to you!' said Nick. He reached into his pocket and held out a package. 'See this, Mercy? I've brought a big lump of sugar for you. Will that sweeten your temper with me?'

But Mercy scowled. She didn't take the sugar, didn't even look at it. 'You *are* strange to me, Nick.' Her eyes were welling with tears and her mouth wobbled. 'You are dressed in somebody else's clothes and you have stolen sugar from somewhere. And money too! You are telling tales that the gold comes from the King, but I'm not a baby any more, Nick! I am not so easily fooled by your stories as I used to be.'

'I'm not fooling you!'

Mercy crossed her arms tight across her heart. 'You did before. You left me, you did! You didn't tell me anything. You ran away and left me. I didn't know where you were or if you were dead like Mother or anything. Master Binder and Pegg have been kind to me and I like it very well here now.'

Pegg smiled. 'And we are happy for Mercy to stay and be as a daughter to us.'

'Daughter?' Nick jumped up, knocking the stool clattering to the floor. 'You plan to take Mercy from me? To replace your Lucy that died. I won't let you! Mercy is mine!'

'We would happily give you a home too, Nick,' said Pegg, quietly.

'Never!' flared Nick, and he turned on Mercy who shrank pale against Pegg's white apron. 'How could you change so much in such a short time?'

'I have not changed!' said Mercy. 'You are the one that's changed, Nick. I don't like you the way you are now.'

'Nor me you!'

Nick turned as the heat of tears swelled his throat and nose and eyes and he knew that if he opened his mouth again it would be a sob that came out. He ran then, out from that clean kitchen and its good smells into the heat and stink and crowded cramped lanes of London. And he felt emptier and more alone than he had ever known it was possible to be. Now I truly have nobody, he thought. I have lost Mercy as surely as if the plague had taken and killed her. London has found another way to take her from me by making her love the Binders better than she loves me. I have no family, no home, no work, no friends. Nick stood still. He took a deep breath to try to steady himself and he looked up from the monochrome London lane to the pure blue sky above, and he saw the ravens and remembered. Yes, he did have one friend in the world, even if that friend was a bird rather than a person. And that friend was another that the King wanted to kill. Nick clenched his fists tight. He turned and ran back towards the Tower.

Chapter Fourteen

As he ran, Nick's mind whirled. How could he save Devil? Trapping the bird to keep him safe wouldn't work. Devil would hate to be trapped more than death itself, and even if Nick kept him captive only for the time it took to carry him out of London, any wild bird would be sure to simply fly home again. Nick imagined Mister Bailey putting out poisoned meat to tempt the birds to death. Or setting soldiers to shoot at the birds and their nests in the walls. What sort of cunning could possibly work against the power of poison or bullets? Nick suddenly remembered what Mercy had said about him trying to fool her with stories. He remembered Lady Robinson winking at him after the incident on the Tower roof. She had said to him, 'Nicholas Raven, you must have spun quite a tale to persuade Sir John from sending you to the colonies. I believe you could talk a person into doing or believing almost anything you cared to make them, you wicked boy!' But he'd not managed to talk Mercy into doing what he wanted. Nick thought hard as he walked back to the Tower.

'Errand done?' asked the guards at the gates.

'Pardon?' said Nick. 'Oh, yes, thank you. I have something for Sir John.' Nick patted his pocket. But the thing he had for Sir John wasn't in any pocket. It was in his mind.

'And where have you been this last hour and more?' demanded Cook as Nick dumped his jacket and bundle in a corner of the kitchen. Mister Bailey is fuming after your guts. He wants help with killing those birds, and I ...'

'Where is he?' asked Nick urgently.

'Gone into the city,' said Cook. 'Now, roll up your sleeves and set to because we've to get to the other side of all this cleaning-up after their grand dinner.'

'Where in the city?' Nick was hopping from foot to foot.

'Who?'

'Mister Bailey, where is he?'

'Oh, he's gone off to the apothecary himself to fetch some poison for those birds since you weren't here to be sent. He'll be back soon enough and then you'll be in for a hiding! Nicholas?'

But Nick had gone already, slipping out of the kitchen and back outside to meet Mister Bailey.

'Where in damnation have you been, Raven?' asked Mister Bailey, handing his package to Nick for him to carry.

'I'm very sorry, Mister Bailey, but I must speak with you,' said Nick, his head dipped humbly. 'I have been out and about in the interests of His Majesty, I assure you.'

Mister Bailey stopped still and put his hands on his hips. 'Not that tale again, surely!'

'But it's true, Sir!' said Nick. 'I went to make sure that I had it all correct and then I hurried to help you, Sir, and to tell you why it is that Devil, I mean the ravens, must not be killed, Sir.'

'Nonsense! The King himself ordered …'

'Oh, I know it,' said Nick. I heard him say the words myself. And I heard that Sir John had given the task of killing the birds to you. But, you see, Mister Bailey, Sir, His Majesty doesn't understand the importance of those birds to his own and his country's place in things.'

'Ha! And you do, I suppose!' Mister Bailey snatched the package back from Nick and began to walk off fast towards the house. Nick scurried after him.

'You see, Sir, it would bring very great calamity to His Majesty if those birds were to die. And you are the only person who can save the King from that calamity.'

'The calamity would be, I suppose, that you would lose that bird that you are fond of. Isn't that right?' Mister Bailey put out a hand to push open the door and Nick hurried to open it for him and then hold the door open in such a way that Mister Bailey couldn't easily slip past.

'His Majesty doesn't see it any more than you do at present,' said Nick. I know why. His Majesty lives so apart from the people. But you, Sir, you know what year we are living in?'

'Of course I do, boy! It is 1666. I'm quite sure that the King knows that as well as I!'

'But haven't you heard the talk?' asked Nick.

Mister Bailey frowned. 'You mean that nonsense they tell about three sixes in a row signifying the sign of the Beast, the Devil, and the end of all things? I don't believe such stuff, and I'm sure that His Majesty doesn't either.' Then Mister Bailey suddenly laughed. 'Oh, I have it now! Because you call that bird of yours after the Devil and he is about to meet his end, that all fits very neatly, does it not!'

'No!' Nick's show of being a humble servant slipped and he let his indignation show. 'That's not it at all, Sir!'

'What is IT then?' Mister Bailey raised one eyebrow. Nick scowled back.

'In all the hundreds of years that this Tower has stood fortress for the kings of England, there has been only one time when the ravens have left the Tower. Do you know when that was, Mister Bailey?'

'Um …'

'It was between the years of 1649 and 1660.'

Mister Bailey shrugged. 'Those were the years when the Lord Protector and his son ruled His Majesty's land. So what is the significance of that?'

'So,' said Nick, 'Those were the years after the first King Charles had his head chopped off, the years when the King's soldiers were used against his own son, our present King Charles. The only time in history when the monarchy did not have rule over this land was also the only time in history when the ravens went from the Tower. Do you see the connection?'

'So you believe …?'

'That the ravens in some way guard the Tower

and guard His Majesty and His Majesty's interests. The times match exactly.'

Mister Bailey looked back over his shoulder towards the White Tower, shading his eyes as he looked up, searching for the birds. 'Well, it's a nonsensical notion, but the connection is there,' he admitted. 'I can't truly believe that such verminous birds could hold power over a king, but the coincidence is certainly odd. And Sir John's position here might depend upon those birds, if you begin to believe what you tell me about the King's fate echoing that of the birds.'

'And your position too, Sir,' said Nick. 'Truly, Mister Bailey, it is most important that Sir John and the King are told. Certainly the birds must not be harmed until the idea has been put to them. Just think how it would be for you if you were the one to kill the birds that held the health and wealth of the King and the nation in their power! Why, Mister Bailey, this could make the difference between your being regarded as a villain on one hand, or a hero on the other.'

'Hero?' said Mister Bailey, patting his wig.

'Indeed!' said Nick. 'Sir John would not listen to my telling such a tale. He has lost all faith in me.'

'That is certainly true,' said Mister Bailey. 'And we all know why that is!'

'But if you were to tell him, Mister Bailey, Sir, how the fate of the Tower and the King and the very nation depends upon those ravens staying safe at the Tower. Well, naturally Sir John would take a great deal of notice of what you tell him, Sir. I dare say that he might even reward you for saving him from the disaster that would have followed if you had used that poison you have there!'

Mister Bailey looked in puzzlement at the package of poison in his hand, then he handed it to Nick. 'I shall go to Sir John and tell him at once,' he said, and he hurried to find his master. He didn't see the grin on Nick's face behind him.

Nick watched Mister Bailey go. And I should hurry too and clean those pots, he thought, or Cook will be after me. I shall work tonight and watch to see if Sir John believes the story, then I will go to Mercy again tomorrow and be clever in what I say to her this time.

A short time later, as Nick stepped out amongst the long shadows of evening to fetch water for Cook, there was a flurry at the door and out came Sir John, mopping his brow and calling for Mister Bailey to follow him.

'Bailey! Are you sure that those precious birds are safe? Where are they? I can see none! Gracious, what am I to do?'

'If you look into the sky, Sir John, you will see them flying as is their habit at this time of day.'

'Yes, I see them, Bailey! Praise God they are safe!'

Nick smiled to himself. If I can woo such an important man as Sir John to do my bidding against the wishes of the King, then surely I can charm my little sister to see things my way too and she can find safety away from London with me.

Later, as the night darkened and dimmed London from view, Nick came out again, bringing scraps of meat.

'Devil?' he called. 'Here, boy! Kraack!'

And down swooped the bird, big and strong and hungry and very much alive. Nick hunkered down and offered Devil scrap after scrap. 'Eat your fill,' he told Devil. I can't bring more because tomorrow I'll be gone, out of London and into the countryside. I shall find work harvesting, if I can. Maybe you'll fly out and join me in the open?' Devil tipped back his head and swallowed, then strode towards Nick. He poked his big-beaked head forward to Nick's knee, and for a moment Nick wondered whether he was about to be pecked as the King had been. But Devil turned his head to one side and simply leaned the side of it against Nick. It was an intimate gesture and Nick felt his eyes filling as he gently stroked a finger over the tufted top of the bird's head and down his strong back. 'I shan't miss London, but I shall miss you,' said Nick. 'You have helped me before, you strange bird. Can't you use your magical powers to rid us all of London?'

'Kraak.'

Nick ruffled Devil's feather top-knot and hugged the bird's body against him with one hand. The bird seemed to wobble in Nick's vision because Nick had tears in his eyes.

Chapter Fifteen

That night was hot. Nick tangled in his bed cover and his thoughts tangled too. When sleep came at last, it was in nightmare form, bringing him visions of London as a plague monster devouring his Mother and reaching out for Mercy. Nick woke, panting and sweating.

'No!'

He must save Mercy. He must, in spite of her wishes. Nick got up from his pallet on the floor and began to dress in the dark. None of the other boys was stirring yet and Nick was glad of that. I'll go now, he decided, before the household is awake. He would tell some fib or other to get through the Tower gates and into London. Then I'll fetch Mercy, he thought. It will be hard to get out through the city gates without a Bill of Health, but I'll think of some story to take us through. Then we'll find a good place to be.

But somebody else was already up, despite

the hour and it being a Sunday. Nick could hear footsteps. And there was another sound that fitted with it being Sunday but was still somehow wrong in a way that made Nick's hot back prickle with unease. He paused in pulling on his shoes. What was it that was wrong? The church bells were ringing too early. And they were ringing bottom-to-top, the notes climbing upwards instead of tumbling downwards in their usual waterfall of noise. Nick felt excitement join fear inside him. Those bells were an alarm call to the city. Nick hurriedly tied his shoes and went out into the corridor to see who it was whose footsteps he had heard and to find out why the alarm was ringing.

Mister Bailey was there, hurrying and tugging his wig into place. 'Raven!' he said, surprised. 'Good boy. The rest are all still asleep. Do you hear the bells?'

'What is it, Sir?' asked Nick. 'Are the Dutch coming up the river to fight us? I don't hear guns.'

'No. There's a fire in the city and I'm told it's a fierce one.' Mister Bailey hurried up the stairs and Nick followed. 'No danger to us here,' said Mister Bailey. 'But Sir John may well be called upon to offer soldiers to help down in the streets.'

Nick stopped still. He hadn't completely shaken off his nightmare about London devouring what he loved. 'Which part is it that is on fire, Sir?'

'All down Fish Street and the lanes round about, I believe,' said Mister Bailey.

'Oh, that's all right then.' Mercy was safely streets away from danger.

Mister Bailey looked sharply at Nick. 'It isn't 'all right' for the fish stall holders, and it isn't 'all right' for our prospects for fish for breakfast!'

'No, of course,' said Nick. 'Are you going to wake Sir John now and tell him?'

'Not yet, I think. And you leave Master James be for the moment. I'm going up the White Tower to see the extent of the thing before I report to Sir John. Do you want to come?' Nick was surprised to see something that was almost friendly about Mister Bailey's face. He could see that Mister Bailey was feeling excitement at the prospect of the fire, just as he was.

'Those are strange sounds, are they not?' said Mister Bailey, and as Nick followed him out of the house and across the courtyard the bells came louder and Nick could hear the giant heartbeat of drums too.

They climbed the White Tower in the shadow

of passing night and they came out onto the roof to see the morning sun pinking the rim of the sky on one side, and another, more orange, light like a second sunrise on the other side of the Tower. There was a wind that blew Nick's hair into his face, but when he pushed the hair aside he saw the raw gash of fire all along the road that led from London Bridge. For a moment neither he nor Mister Bailey said anything. They watched London, shrunk small as a toy by distance, but clearly alive because the fire moved and smoked and they could hear it and smell it as well as see it. Then Mister Bailey said quietly. 'That is a mighty big fire. And a good many buildings lost. I was told that over 200 buildings are feared burned already, and many more ablaze now by the look of it. Still, the Tower should stand firm with those birds to protect it, eh?'

'Yes, Sir,' said Nick, smiling inside at the joke of Mister Bailey's belief in his story. He felt strangely happy, watching London burn. 'Look!' He pointed to where the ravens were flying over the fire, seeming to stir it from above, fanning it with their wings. Like tiny witches on broomsticks, thought Nick, and he loved them for it. For once it was London itself that was in pain and being destroyed. Not just destroyed, but cleansed too. The Lord Mayor had had them all make fires in the streets in an attempt to kill off the plague, but that burning had not been enough. Perhaps this great fire could make things properly clean?

Nick felt a kind of glory and power and happiness in those surging flames, but he heard Mister Bailey saying, 'This wind will blow the fire as a bellows would blow a smithy's fire. It will spread away from us, I thank the Lord, but it will be a job to stop its progress when everything is so tinder-dry through lack of rain.'

'Which direction will it spread?' asked Nick.

'It is being sent westwards.' Mister Bailey pointed. 'See? Already it is advancing.'

Towards Shoe Lane, thought Nick, and he suddenly saw the blackness of the smoke and the length of the fire spread like a wall between where he was and where Mercy must soon be in danger, and he felt sick.

'Please, Mister Bailey,' asked Nick. 'How could a person get past that fire?'

Mister Bailey looked sharply at Nick. 'Do you have family close by?'

'My sister,' said Nick, and he pointed in the direction of Shoe Lane, already hidden beneath a smudge of black smoke. Nick suddenly felt as if he was choking on that smoke, even though the wind blew fresh from behind them. He looked into Mister Bailey's face. 'Please, Sir, might I go to her?'

'I think that you must,' said Mister Bailey, startled to see sincerity in the boy. I will inform Sir John. You would do best to take a boat, although many others will have the same idea and a place in a boat might be hard to find. On second thoughts, perhaps you would do better to go north, above the fire, and skirt it that way. Go now, boy, and see your sister safe.'

'Thank you, Mister Bailey, Sir,' said Nick. 'Thank you very much,' and he was already running for the stairs.

Nick didn't have his bundle of belongings, didn't have his golden coin with him, but none of that mattered. All that mattered was to get past the fire and to find Mercy.

Chapter Sixteen

As Nick ran down into the city, the sharp smell of the fire made breathing hard, and he was soon gasping for what little goodness he could take from the air. The heat and his running made sweat trickle down his back with a feeling like ants crawling. And all the time it got hotter. There were people running, screaming and stumbling away from the fire, carrying whatever possessions they could save. Nick saw some with scarlet burns on faces and hands, saw an old woman collapsed and carried by two others, saw a small child standing alone, big-eyed and wailing for his mother who wasn't there. He saw a sick old man being carried on a bed. Nick passed them all by because his mind was on Mercy, small frail Mercy who might be lying poisoned by smoke and maybe not even yet woken to this terrible morning.

Then, round a corner, Nick came to the flames. He put up his hands to shield his face from the furnace heat, and his head throbbed with the weird wild roaring sound of the flames as the wind pushed them up and into and over the buildings. Flames reached up above five-storey buildings, up into the sky, and rags of flame flew up and leapt the buildings to spread the fire nearer and nearer to Mercy. Nick turned and ran the streets and lanes which were not alight, trying desperately to get around the fire. He stumbled and tripped and he gasped for breath as he used his hands and arms to push through the crowds running the other way. Rich and poor alike were running for their lives, and Nick saw that they were all the same, all smut-blinded, cinder-choked and their homes gone. London was loud with the sounds of wailing and shouting, the roar of the flames and the backwards bells, the crashing of falling roofs, and the explosions of barrels of tar and oil. Nick ran over cobbles so hot they burned through the thick leather soles of his shoes. All around were piles of collapsed buildings, all black and white ash with occasional flaring sores of small fires, and the air was poison to breath. Nick pulled his shirt up over his mouth and hurried. Ash blew white specks in the wind like a blizzard. Like winter, yet hot as Hell. Life was turned upside down. Nick fought the heat and the noise and the people to come at last to Shoe Lane.

Mercy.

Through streaming eyes Nick saw the whirling orange flames filling the lane, the wind whipping them high to gobble all they could. Nick could feel the power of it. The wind sucked the air from his lungs, and pulled him towards the flames too.

'No!' But if it could almost pull Nick off his feet, then what would it do to a small Mercy with no weight to anchor her? Nick's legs shook, but he ran up the lane. His mouth and throat were parched dry. 'Mercy!'

Nick could see the Binders' small house, its door agape as if the house was panting to breathe in that heat. But the fire was racing too, pouring up the lane like water down a stream, and halting Nick with its heat. He bent and chewed the air, trying to find the breath he needed to prevent himself from collapsing. Because he knew that if anybody was still in Seth Binder's home, there was no way to save them now, from the poisoned air, from the flames, from the destruction all around. It was too late.

Nick stepped back and away from the lane until

his heaving lungs could breathe and his pounding head could think a little. He leaned against a house wall, and he sobbed. Then something banged into him, knocking him down to the ground. He looked up at a hand cart, loaded with goods, at more people running for their lives. Might Mercy have run too? Would Pegg and Seth have heard the bells and the commotion and the fire itself and got out of the house in time? What time of day was it now anyway? Nick couldn't guess whether minutes or hours had passed since he stood above it all on the White Tower with Mister Bailey and felt the fire to be glorious. Nick thought of the Binders' door, hanging open. If they had escaped, then he might still find his sister.

So Nick joined the throngs of shocked, desperate people trying to get away from the fire. He joined a stream of people heading down to the river where every boat was afloat and filled with people and furniture and animals and all were shouting and crying. Nick elbowed his way to the water's edge that was high with the tide, and he dipped in scooped hands and drank the brown river water. He splashed it on his face and sank his wrists into it. The taste was salty-foul and Nick knew that it might make him ill, but he had to drink. Then he went searching the crowds, hunting the faces for Mercy or Pegg or Seth. The people kept coming, swarming from the city as ants will pour forth if you cut their ant hill open with a spade. Nick had never been in such a crowd of people, nor felt so completely alone.

Was the sky darkening with night or was it just the mass of black smoke? Nick couldn't tell. Great explosions rocked the air. 'That's the tar blowing up,' said somebody.

'No, it isn't,' said another. 'It's the French guns. They're invading!'

'Was it them that started the fire then?' asked the first man.

'Most likely was,' said the second.

Had the war really come into London, wondered Nick? Nick spun, looking north, south, east, west. Which way might the Binders have fled? Could Mercy still be saved?

''Tis the end of the world for all to see,' wailed a woman. And that is just how it felt to Nick as he pushed back into the crowds, back towards the fire, looking, looking for Mercy.

In the fog of smoke and showering of white ash that fell gently like hot snow, Nick bent over like an old man. Church towers were tumbling now, their great bells crashing their last notes as they fell. Nick needed water again, but every public water stand was dried up. In the livid orange light of flames leaping into the sky streets away, Nick saw great buildings and small homes all crumpling and falling as the fire growled and pounced and raged through the city. Nick folded over, gasping for breath as the fire danced with manic glee in the streets around him. He tried to feel his rage against London and the King to give him the strength to keep going, keep him looking for Mercy. But there seemed nothing left inside him to care very much about anything. He wanted to close his eyes and just let everything stop.

Nick did close his eyes and heard other sounds as well as the roar and wail and rumble of the fire. He could hear shouting and the irregular beat of many mallets and picks. Nick blinked his stinging eyes and looked up to see a group of men and a few women who weren't running from the fire at all. Instead they were joining in with the fire's destruction, pulling down good houses that the fire had not yet touched.

'You're gone mad!' shouted Nick, his anger suddenly returned. He ran at one man and tried to take the pickaxe from him. The man shrugged Nick off and laughed.

'We don't need to fight you as well, young one! If you've got strength to spare, then you'd do best to join us.'

The man put a hand on Nick's shoulder and kindly explained. They were taking down buildings to make a fire break of bare earth that the fire wouldn't be able to cross. 'It's the only way to halt her,' said the man. He winked at Nick and added, 'Besides, we're getting paid by the King and his brother to do this, you know. They're very keen that the fire shouldn't reach their own palaces and parks. Stick around and they'll come by again and tell us all to work harder, I wouldn't wonder.'

'The King?'

'None other than His Majesty King Charles the Second himself.'

Somehow the thought that the King might come to that place made Nick stay. He settled behind the man, pulling clear the timbers that the man had pickaxed free. Sweating and exhausted, he dragged the heavy timbers to the far end of the street. Then Nick took a turn with the pick, swinging and hauling and lifting. It was good to have a purposeful job, a way to fight the fire to try to give Mercy a chance to escape. Nick smashed and pulled and dragged on and on. Was it for minutes or hours or days? He didn't know. Then a clatter of hooves on cobbles came as a new sound into his numbed mind. Out of the sooty darkness came two figures on horseback, lit intermittently by the flickering flame-light. Nick looked at the boots in stirrups that came level with his bent head and he slowly thought what very fine boots they were. Something nudged at Nick's arm. It was a leather water bottle being offered.

'A drink?' asked a man's voice, and Nick grasped the bottle and tipped it and drank great gulps before he realised that what he drank was something very much stronger than water. The man laughed. 'That will do you good!' Nick could feel something powerful running through him and he smiled and knew that he was a little drunk. He looked up to a beaky nose and raven black eyes and hair and a thin moustache, and Nick laughed.

'You're the King!' he said, giggling. Suddenly everything seemed funny. Nick laughed again. 'I have hated the King,' he told the tall man on the horse, and he giggled some more.

'I have hated myself often enough,' said the King. 'But now we must both hate this fire enough to extinguish it, don't you think? I will pay for work well done.'

'Thank you,' said Nick, and he bowed his head just slightly.

Chapter Seventeen

After that, time lost any meaning to Nick. At first he thought it was the drink in him that made the normal order of everything so utterly changed. Perhaps it was all a dream and only in his head, and that was why the King acted in a way that no real king would surely act, serving drinks to scruffy boys? But the heat and the noise and work were real enough. And more than once the King was there, working alongside the people as they used grappling hooks, picks, hammers, rakes, bare hands and booted feet to pummel and pull down buildings, to clear away the rubble and leave bare earth that a fire could not cross.

As Nick sobered he felt himself flooding with sadness. Maybe it was the smoke, but his eyes streamed. His family was all gone, and now London was dying too, and suddenly he minded that very much. That new fury powered Nick to keep hacking and pulling and kicking and cursing as he and the others fought the fire together. Again and again they saw the fire leap the roof tops and spread beyond the fire break they had just made. But, with shouts of rage, they picked up their tools and ran and began all over again, trying, trying to get ahead of the fire and defeat it.

Day seemed the same as night because the smoke was so thick. And night seemed like day because the giant flames made such a great bonfire of the city. It made lanterns of churches, flames flickering at their windows. St Paul's made the biggest lantern of them all as the stores of books inside it burnt, and then the building itself gave in to the fire and died. Cobblestones and stores of oils exploded like fireworks. Nick's ears rang from the noise of it all. What had been solid turned to liquid, with glass windows and lead piping melting to run down the gutters. Nick was burnt raw and bruised and scratched. There was no fooling a fire by playing a part, no fooling this enemy into doing your bidding.

Nick's mood swung from fury to despair to anger again until he didn't even know how he felt about anything any more. The fire boiled water in the wells and baked the plague dead in their graves. Nick thought of his mother as he raked smouldering timbers and doused the sparks that flew on the wind like stars. He was glad that she wasn't here to witness the horror of all this, glad that her diseased body would be burned away and gone entirely to leave his memories of her clean. Nick hacked and tugged and destroyed, all in order to save his city and his sister. I might be going mad, he thought.

The work went on and on. As the hours passed, Nick sat with bread in his hand and fell asleep without tasting it. He was too dry and too tired to chew anything. He didn't know how long the sleep lasted, but he woke and worked again for what seemed an eternity before sleeping and waking again. Would it ever end? The fire has won, thought Nick more than once. But then the King or his brother the Duke came again, filthy and tired themselves. They got down off their horses to work alongside the common people with such energy that Nick knew that he could not after all surrender to the fire just yet.

Once, as Nick rested and tried to eat some mutton and bread handed to him, there suddenly boomed an explosion of such force that Nick felt it in his chest and throat and pounding his ears.

'They're blowing up the houses now. Got the

military onto it at last. Maybe that'll give us a chance,' said a man. Nick covered his ears and waited for the next explosion to hit. He shut his eyes against the blast and ducked, imagining falling tiles and bricks, but it was something soft that came with a faint freshness of a breeze to land on his shoulder.

'Kraack!'

The meat was snatched from his fingers.

'Devil!'

Just as it had seemed to Nick that Devil and the other birds had stirred and fanned the flames when he had seen them from the Tower that first morning of the fire, so now it seemed to Nick that Devil was acting with a purpose. Why had he flown over those miles of fire to Nick? The bird stretched its wings and flapped, shaking off soot and cooling itself, and Nick noticed the taste of something fresher in the breeze flapped by the bird's wings. Then Devil stretched wide his wings, holding them still as he rose up easily on the hot air, higher and higher, straight upwards.

'The wind, it's changing!' shouted somebody.

Nick looked up and saw that the sparks that had come at them and over them hour after hour, day after day, were floating straight upwards now, just as Devil was. And, as Devil pointed the way towards the Tower and flapped for home, the sparks too began to turn in the air, heading back towards the fire.

'Smoke's turning away! The fire will consume itself. Praise be to God for some mercy at last!'

That word 'mercy' struck Nick like a hammer blow. Was his Mercy dead or alive?

All around Nick, exhausted men stopped their smashing and raking and found the energy for talk now that the danger seemed to be dwindling.

'Of course the Tower's under threat now that the fire's turned,' said somebody. 'Think of all the munitions in there and the firework show we'll get from that!'

'I have friends in the Tower,' said Nick quietly, getting to his feet.

'More birds, is it?' laughed the man beside him.

'People too,' said Nick.

'Well, leave the Tower to others, I say,' said the man. 'We've every one of us done all that anybody could ask of a man and more.'

'I'm going there,' said Nick, a sore hand to his bruised sweaty forehead. James and Lady Robinson, Sir John, Cook and even Mister Bailey were in his thoughts. He was surprised to realise that he cared about them all. 'I must help them.'

'Then why not beg a lift down the river with His Majesty!' laughed another. 'He's over there, look, and I heard that he's heading for the Tower now.'

Chapter Eighteen

It just seemed another part of the new normality that Nick was sitting in a hired boat alongside the King, being rowed down the broad River Thames that had become a soup of floating furniture and cases and people in boats of all kinds. They sat side by side, tall man and tall boy, each dark and filthy with soot. Everybody in that boat was blackened. They seemed to be silhouette people. Nick looked across to the bank where he could see that the great buildings of London had crumbled to stubs like bad teeth. Flames quarrelled with themselves in the shifting wind. Nick and King Charles sat in silence, trying to take in the extent of the devastation, and letting the river cool them a little. There was horror in what they saw, but there was also beauty in the great flames that glinted like jewels and reflected in the river to show it all double, above and below the line of riverbank. A heaven and a hell of London, thought Nick.

He looked toward the Tower, still standing firm and strong beyond the wreckage, and he saw how the flames were licking, flickering towards that direction now, pinking the White Tower. But above the White Tower there were dark specs in the sky above; ravens flying.

'All will be well with the Tower,' he told the King.

King Charles turned to the boy beside him. 'What makes you so sure of that?'

'The ravens, Your Majesty. Do you see them? They haven't left the Tower. They would leave if they felt danger there, do you not think? They could fly wherever they wished to fly, but they've chosen to stay at the Tower. That means that Your Majesty and the Tower will stay strong.' Nick was surprised to realise that he was no longer telling this as a story. He felt it to be true.

The King's black eyebrows showed puzzlement.

'There is a power in the ravens, Your Majesty,' said Nick.

'Who are your family?' asked the King. 'Do I know you? You seem somehow familiar.'

The tug-tug of the boat being rowed was calming. Nick answered the King simply. 'My Father is dead in the war. My mother dead of the plague.' The thought of Mercy made his heart sore within his chest.

'My own parents are dead too,' said the King, and Nick looked at him. The man seemed more like a sad sort of boy than a King just then. 'And two dear sisters of mine are dead of the smallpox and a small brother also dead before his time. I don't know why God let them die and not me. I have been in the path of death often enough.'

'I have lost my sister,' said Nick quietly. 'I think she might be dead too.' He felt his lips wobble, so he pressed them firmly together again.

The boat bumped softly against the landing stage and the King rose up, tall and dark and suddenly every inch a King once more, in spite of his scruffy appearance. 'Come,' he said, setting off towards the Tower with long strides, his tatty courtiers following behind. The King gave Nick a kindly look, back over his shoulder. 'One more battle to fight, to save my Tower. Maybe your birds really will help. I remember you now. You are the boy who minded the ravens and dogs at the Tower.'

'I am,' said Nick, and he ran on wobbly legs to catch up with the long strides of the King. He wondered quite what he felt about that man and this place now, and he didn't know the answer.

Everything was in commotion within the Tower walls. They found Sir John Robinson in tattered shirt sleeves, scarlet-faced and shouting orders. All around him rushed soldiers and servants carrying goods. Like ants carrying their fat white baby bundles to safety from a broken nest, thought Nick. When Sir John suddenly spotted Nick limping toward him, he seemed to swell. Sir John's chins wobbled. He pointed a plump finger at Nick. 'Raven!' Sir John took a step towards Nick and shouted, 'You, boy! You were allowed by Mister Bailey to go and fetch your sister, but not to abscond for four whole days and nights! Here, we have had no sleep to speak of and precious little rest and every old woman and young child has been doing their damnedest to save His Majesty's belongings while you, you who should have been here to serve your masters, have disappeared just when you were most needed. And then you return, hoping for your job back, I dare say. Well, not this time, Raven! You are finished at the Tower and nothing that my silly soft wife or son say in your defence can save you from being handed to the navy this time!'

The tall dark bedraggled figure standing beside

Nick took a step closer. 'My dear Robinson, what if your silly soft King was to say something in the boy's defence?'

'Oh, Your Majesty!' Sir John, tattered and stained and sweaty, swept a perfect low bow. 'Your Majesty, forgive me, I did not recognise you. I …'

'Stand up straight, man! I realise that I do not quite look the part of the monarch, but, as you so eloquently put it, every damned old woman and child has been helping to fight the fire and you can add every damned king to that list too. Your bird boy has been working for me, taking down buildings to halt the fire westwards. Thirsty work.' The King raised a dark eyebrow towards a servant girl who scuttled off to find drinks for the royal visitor. 'I have instructed that the sailors be put to blowing up the buildings close to the Tower walls. So prepare yourself for the noise of it and relax a little. Let us share some refreshment to celebrate the worst of it being over. By the look of you, you have need of a drink as much as I!'

So it was that Sir John and the King sat on a low wall that was sheltered from the worst of the smoke, and waited for the girl to arrive with drinks. Nick and an assortment of courtiers stood awkwardly beside them. Nick looked up at the dark smoke stroking the fortress of the White Tower while the birds circled above. The King seemed content, but Sir John was not. He stood up and began bowing.

'You must come into the house, please Your Majesty. My good lady wife will want to entertain you more fittingly. It really is not suitable for you out here.'

King Charles raised a hand. 'Your good lady wife will have a fit of the vapours if I walk into her house and she is not prepared for me, as well you know. No, I thank you, Robinson, but I prefer to sit in the air, even if there is no escape from this damned smoke that makes the eyes water. You offer your finest, and I thank you for that. But wine is not the drink to quench a real thirst. Today is a day for all to be different. Ale and lots of it is what I crave.' Sir John shifted uneasily from foot to foot, distressed to have the King not behaving as a King should.

'Should I show Your Majesty what …'

'No,' said the King, holding up a hand. Not now. We are all weary beyond checking on this and that just now. Good Sir John, I suggest that you go to your house and make yourself more comfortable. I am very content to sit in peace for a while.'

'I? Go and change? Why, yes, to be sure,' said Sir John, and off he bustled, only turning to scowl at Nick who, without thinking, had sat himself down next to the King as the girl arrived with a jug and glasses. She was far cleaner and smarter than the King she served.

Chapter Nineteen

They sat on the wall, swallowing ale and munching apples and bread and cheese and meat. The King gazed at the billowing sky full of sparks and smoke while Nick watched him, looking curiously at the man that he had hated for so long. I have the chance now to say anything I want to, thought Nick. I could take up that fruit knife and attack him if I chose to. But the hatred was gone. Nothing was left but sorrow for what had gone from his life, and hollow dread for what might have happened to Mercy. The King, too, seemed to have lost much. Nick looked at him curiously. But, weary and filthy, the King did not seem distressed. He looked as if he had found some kind of calm in the chaos they had just lived through.

'Your Majesty, do you care very much that such a lot of London has been destroyed?' asked Nick.

King Charles took a deep breath and tipped his

head back. 'Well, many old friends are gone forever. St Paul's, the Exchange, and, oh, so much more.' He swept a hand from left to right. 'All gone.' He leaned forward, resting elbows on knees. Then he twisted his head to Nick and Nick saw a spark of excitement in the King's bloodshot and exhausted eyes. 'But do you see the opportunity that this gives us now? A chance to build a new London, a better London! I have thought of making London a finer place before, but the landowners in the city did not like the idea. Now we shall have to build anew, whatever their view. And we shall build with beauty, don't you think? If the people live in a place of beauty, then they will be less inclined to quarrel, I'm sure of it. Out of this terror will come peace, I hope.'

A great explosion crumped the air all around and echoed off the Tower's many stone walls.

'Good,' said the King. 'My brother is seeing that all is done as it should be.' He yawned, then blinked his eyes and peered at Nick. 'Good gracious, whatever have you got on your shoulder?'

'My raven,' said Nick.

'Kraack!' called Devil.

'Kraack,' Nick replied.

'You speak fluent raven?' laughed the King.

'Then do ask him what he wants of us.'

'He has noticed the food,' said Nick. 'And maybe the glint of the knife.'

The King chuckled. 'I do believe he's the very bird that went for my ankles, is he not? Well, I should be safe today because nothing at all sparkles on me now!'

Nick liked the feel of Devil's strong claws clasping his shoulder, his soft feathers against the side of his face, even though the bird was heavy and Nick so tired. He fed Devil titbits, passing them up to keep him there awhile.

'Do you think that the fire will see the end of the plague?' asked Nick.

The King shrugged. 'Maybe so. Then that will be another goodness to come from bad. This is a strange world, is it not, Raven?' Another explosion pressed the air onto their ears and made them spill their drinks. 'Lord, why do I jump when I know very well what they are doing?' laughed the King. 'And, see, that bird of yours doesn't stir a feather at it! Remarkable things, birds. I have a great collection of them.'

'You commanded that this raven should be killed,' said Nick, a little daring.

'Did I really? Then I must have been in a foul

temper over something. I'm really very fond of birds of all sorts, especially clever ones and loyal ones. Creatures of all kinds are often more honest companions than people, I find. London is full of those who pretend to like me, but do not,' said the King.

Nick put a bit of meat on the ground to tempt Devil down from his shoulder. He told the King, 'I have hated London these last years.'

'Oh, I know that feeling well!' said the King. 'And London has hated me back, very often. And yet I wanted to fight to save it from the fire, so I must have a fondness for it too. Have you family in the city?'

Nick swallowed. 'I might have my sister still,' he said. If she has survived the fire. The house where she was is burned, and I fear that she must be dead. I had wanted to take her from London, to go and live safe in the countryside.'

King Charles looked kindly down on Nick. 'We cannot yet begin to know who has survived this fire. I am afraid that some have indeed died. But if your sister escaped, then she has very likely gone to the Moore Fields. That is where many thousands have fled. I have seen them myself, and I have instructed that the people round about should help to feed and house the homeless if they can.'

'The Moore Fields,' said Nick, getting to his feet. 'I must go there then, and look for her.' He wobbled on his feet and he had to put a hand to the wall to steady himself.

'Slowly, boy!' said the King. 'Rest and refresh yourself before you set out. We are each of us only human!'

Sir John, hastily clean and bewigged but still scarlet in the face, came bustling over and bowed low before the King. 'Ah, I see that you have made friends with our ravens, Your Majesty. You will note that they are still alive in spite of your orders, but that is all for very good reason, I assure you. I must explain that if the ravens were to leave the Tower it would bring great bad luck to Your Majesty and to all of us. Truly, Your Majesty, we must never allow those ravens to leave the Tower.'

Nick hid a smile as he heard his own story being told by Sir John. But Sir John suddenly noticed Nick sitting there and he tugged at the neck of Nick's filthy shirt. 'How dare you sit there as if you were His Majesty's equal, Raven! Get up at once! Get out of my sight!'

The King held up a hand. 'But by your own

admission, Robinson, we mustn't allow ravens to leave the Tower. That is the boy's name, is it not? Raven?'

'Ha! Very droll, Your Majesty.' Sir John's mouth twitched uncomfortably. Nick suddenly felt in a mood for honesty. He stood respectfully and said, 'Your Majesty has it wrong.'

'How dare you accuse His Ma…!' began Sir John, but the King put a hand onto Sir John's arm to quiet him and allow Nick to finish.

'My true name is not Raven, Sir.'

'What?' Sir John was inflating once more.

'I am Nicholas Truelove. I played a part when I came to your home, Sir John. I am sorry for that.'

Boom! Another explosion, louder than the others, meant that none heard what Sir John's opening and closing mouth was saying to that.

Chapter Twenty

Sir John, flattered into kindness by the King, turned anger into generosity when all was explained.

'It seems that you have served well, after all, young man,' he told Nick. And, whatever your name, all families should try to find each other after a catastrophe such as this. Go to the house, Raven. Take some rest. Then go and seek your sister.'

'Thank you, Sir ...' began Nick, but Sir John waved away the thanks.

'Tell Cook to give you food for your journey. I wish you well for all that you are a scoundrel and a knave!'

Nick was so tired and stiff that he could hardly stand and walk as far as the Robinson's house. His mind was muddled with exhaustion. He curled into his corner of the kitchen and slept and then woke and washed. Cook gave him the promised food. James sneaked down into the kitchen to shake Nick's hand and wish him well.

'Come back with your sister when you find her,' he said.

But Nick shook his head. 'She's likely dead, Master James. I won't be coming back to London with or without her. But give my thanks to your parents for their kindness, will you, please?'

The Robinson house was full of friends and family who had lost houses to the fire and needed a place for them and their belongings to stay. Nick felt a little guilty not to be staying to help at such a busy time, but if there was any chance that Mercy could be found, he must follow it. He slipped through the busy streets of the Tower, alone except for Devil who came down to land at his feet just outside the Tower gate. Nick bent and touched the top of the raven's head.

'Those feathers hardly stick up at all now,' he said. 'That means that you are growing up.' The raven put his head on one side.

'Kraack!'

'I'm going,' said Nick. But you are safe now that the King has trust in you. Look after him, Devil. If you don't, you will make me even more of a liar than I have been!'

Then Nick walked into the hot black and white world of smouldering London, skirting around the places where the fire still flared with life. He headed north, plunging back into the hellish twilight world of a smoke-black sky lit by fires below. There were no shadows to mark the hours in London now, no stopping for meals to mark the time. Eyes stinging and weeping from the smoke, lungs raw from gasping in the smoky air, Nick ran and walked and ran again amongst the colourless people carrying their lives and loved ones and all going the same way. For hours he walked. The crowd got bigger the nearer he got to the city walls and the gate. They were grey, these people, and they wailed their despair at all they had lost. Nick kept going as fast as he could, out through the great gates, with no Bill of Health asked for, out along the road and into the fields. There, the people of London sat and staggered over fields made as grey as themselves by fallen ash, all of them wondering what was to become of them now that their homes and livelihoods had gone, with the year heading towards winter.

Amid the crowd of thousands staggering onwards, heads down, Nick's own head was up and looking, looking for Mercy or Seth or Pegg or even Mistress Jenkins or any other who might know of their whereabouts. But all seemed to be strangers, and how could you spot one small girl amongst such a mass of people, all of them looking the same and all walking the same way? Nick felt his last hope draining away. He stopped still, letting the mass of people pass by all around him. He was suddenly too tired to keep walking. He closed his eyes to ease the stinging pain from the gritty smoke, and he let tears rinse under his eyelids a moment. And he thought of Devil and of how the bird could rise up above humanity and look down and see clear what could not be seen from within such a close-pressed crowd. If only Nick had wings to carry him high into the smudged sky and look down to see that red cap of Mercy's.

The noise around Nick suddenly changed, and he opened his eyes. There were shouts and pointing, and then a strange continuous cry mixing hope and desperation. The crowd veered like a shoal of fish, all turning together to press towards something. Nick looked over a mass of heads to see a group of men on horseback. The tallest of those men was the King, now clean and colourful above the filthy crowd.

'Your Majesty!' shouted Nick. He too began

to push through the crowd, edging and shoving his thin body between others. All around were arms waving and voices calling out love for the King and begging for help. I am just another grey person amongst so many that the King will never see me unless I do something different from the others, thought Nick.

So, as he got near to the horses, Nick put his hands either side of his mouth and called, 'Kraack! Kraack!' The King turned in his saddle, searching the crowd, puzzled. Nick did it again. 'Kraack!'

'Raven? Truelove?'

Nick waved, pushed his way close. 'Your Majesty! Please, Your Majesty, can you see my sister from up there?'

The King laughed kindly. 'I see a great river of people running uphill to flood the fields, but I wouldn't know your sister amongst them all even if I did see her.'

'But she has a red cap,' said Nick.

'Red, you say?' asked the King, then he shook his head in amazement and pointed. 'Then we have a miracle because I see a small girl over there who has a red cap on her head! Could she be your sister?' The King turned and said something to one of his men, who rode his horse through the crowd to bend and pick up the girl and carry her to where Nick stood with the crowd pushing noisily around him. The small girl in the red cap was struggling in the man's arms.

'Put me down at once!'

'Mercy!'

'Nick?'

Nick took Mercy into his arms, and the crowd cheered around them.

At first they just clung together, Mercy and Nick, and they couldn't say anything. Then Nick pushed Mercy away a little. He bent down to her height and blinked his eyes clear of tears to look at her properly. 'Are you well, Mercy?' he said. 'I saw the fire in Shoe Lane ...' Nick shook his head and couldn't say more. Mercy flung herself around Nick again and held on tight.

'Where were you, Nick? I feared for you so!'

Nick chuckled. 'It's for me to worry over you, you little goose. Not the other way round!'

'But you had none to care for you and I had good Seth and Pegg!'

'Lord, I'm glad you're safe,' said Nick. 'And I'm mighty glad that Mistress Binder chose to make your new cap red!' And he rocked her and smelled the smoke in her hair. 'We are out in the country after all and beginning a new life, even though you said that you wouldn't do it!'

'It isn't funny, Nick!'

'No,' agreed Nick. 'It isn't.'

'But look!' said Mercy. She pointed to a cloth-covered button that was odd in its size amongst the buttons that fastened her bodice. She went up on tiptoe and cupped a hand over Nick's ear. 'It's the silver button, still safe, so we do have something to start a new life with.' Nick smiled and patted Mercy's hand. 'That's good,' he said. Nick gently took a stray strand of Mercy's hair between finger and thumb and he pushed it beneath her cap. 'I have been fighting the fire these last days and the King gave me some money in payment, so we have more.'

'The King! I think I saw His Majesty here just now, but …' Mercy looked around. The King had gone. 'Oh, Nick, don't go making up stories again. Please!'

'This isn't a story,' said Nick. I have been in the fire and with the King and his brother. The old London is gone, you know, Mercy. But King Charles told me that they will build London new and better.'

'But who will build it? And where will people live? Where will we go, Nick?'

'I don't know,' said Nick. 'I don't know.'

'Well, I know, even if you do not,' said Mercy. 'We will live with the Binders.'

'They will take you, maybe,' said Nick. 'But ...'

'They will take you too,' said Mercy. They have said so. Seth has said often how he misses your help with his work. You could learn carpenting with Seth and help to make London anew.'

'I'd like to learn to carve wood,' said Nick quietly. The King said that the new London will be made beautiful. I saw wonderful carvings in the Robinson's house at the Tower. Wood carved into flowers and birds that looked as real as if they were natural.'

'The Tower?' said Mercy, puzzled. 'Why were you at the King's Tower? Were you ever really there? Were you a prisoner?'

Nick shook his head. 'Come,' he said. Where did you leave your kind Binders? They will be worrying for you. I will tell you everything once we have found them.'

There was no carving to be done, nor even any proper carpentry that night.

'We must just prop up some kind of shelter with

whatever we have to hand,' said Seth when they found them. 'We'll have some small shelter if we can find any space left alongside that hedge there.' There was little green to be seen under the mass of people, dumped and dismayed and exhausted. All over the fields people were making rough tents from sheeting and cloaks and carts turned on their sides.

''Tis like a scene from the Bible,' said Pegg. 'And I don't know whether to pray for rain to put out the fire in the city or pray for dry weather so that we don't get a soaking tonight. But, whatever it does, we'll all sleep sound. I've never felt more weary nor more strange in all of my life.'

They sat, four corners of a square. 'Quite like a family once more,' said Pegg quietly, and Seth reached out a hand to touch her.

They ate the food that Nick had brought from Cook. 'I do thank your friends at the Tower for this,' said Pegg. 'They must be good people.'

'I think that they are, after all,' agreed Nick with a frown and then a smile that grew into a yawn. He slumped down onto the grass. Mercy took his head onto her lap, and she yawned wide too.

'Tell us the story of it all now, Nick,' she said.

But Nick's eyes had already closed. Mercy

stroked the hair from her brother's face. And she sang softly the old words that Mother had used to sing to him when he was small. And now the words and Mercy's stroking brought into Nick's mind his first clear memory of Mother as she had been before the plague struck. He remembered her kind and happy, and the next yawn turned into a slight smile as Mercy sang:

> 'Nicky Truelove shining bright,
> Lift your wings and take to flight.
> Fly right through the starry night
> Down to land in morning light.
> Darling Nicky Truelove.'

From Pippa Goodhart

If you visit the Tower of London you will find ravens there with their wings clipped to stop them from flying away. There is a Yeoman Raven Master to look after them. If you ask him why ravens are kept like that at the Tower, he will tell you that they are kept there because of a story. That story says that if the ravens ever leave the Tower, then the monarch and the kingdom will fall, and that is why King Charles the Second decreed that there must always be ravens at the Tower.

But historians will tell you that actually that isn't true. There is no written decree or law about the ravens. So nobody really knows where the idea of ravens being important at the Tower comes from. This story about Nick Truelove and his raven friend tells you how I think that story might have come about. The story is fiction, but a lot of what happens in it is true.

Sir John Robinson and his wife and son were

real people. I've taken their characters from what Samuel Pepys tells us about them in his Diary. The way that the Robinsons took Nick into their household may seem unlikely, but it is based on a real event recorded by Pepys. This is what Pepys wrote after having dined with the Robinsons at their home at the Tower of London:

'No discourse at table to any purpose, only after dinner my Lady would needs see a boy which was represented to her to be an innocent country boy brought up to towne a day or two ago, and left here to the wide world, and he losing his way fell into the Tower, which my Lady believes, and takes pity on him, and will keep him; but though a little boy and but young, yet he tells his tale so readily and answers all questions so wittily, that for certain he is an arch rogue, and bred in this towne; but my Lady will not believe it, but ordered victuals to be given him, and I think will keep him as a footboy for their eldest son.'

The bird, Devil, behaves as ravens do in real life. They are very clever birds, often copying what they see other people do and tricking people and other birds. They get attached to particular people and can be trained to behave in certain ways. Like magpies, they like to steal anything bright and shiny.

King Charles the Second was a very interesting man. He fought in bloody battles in the English Civil War when he was only a child. When his father was captured and finally beheaded, Prince Charles had to flee for his life. He lived on the run for many years, often in poverty. He had learnt that grand people weren't always kind to him, and sometimes very poor people risked their own safety to save his life. So, even when he became king, he never took wealth for granted, and he was happy to mix with anybody from any class of people if he liked and trusted them.

When he came back to England to become king, Charles had new crown jewels made and he liked to dress and live very extravagantly. He kept a great collection of birds and dogs. His golden barge was a present from the Doge of Venice. It is illustrated in pictures from the time, and there's a small bit of it on display at the Tower of London. King Charles and his brother, the Duke of York (later King James the Second) really did take an active part in putting out the Great Fire. It made them popular heroes because the people who should have been leading Londoners in their troubles, such as the Lord Mayor of London, did very little to help. The king and his brother worked with anybody who would stay and fight the fire. They rode around, encouraging people to pull down houses and make a fire break. They paid out money to the workers, and they even got down off their horses and joined in with the work themselves. They also rode out to the Moore Fields and did their best to help the people who swarmed there to escape from the fire. When at last the wind changed and the fire turned, the Duke of York supervised the blowing up of houses near the Tower to protect it from the fire. The King had been wanting to make London a more modern city, a bit like Paris, even before the fire destroyed so much. He had already sent Christopher Wren to study cities abroad and to make plans for a new London with a new St Paul's Cathedral. The Great Fire of London burned 373 acres of the city, leaving only 75 acres of the city standing, so there was a lot of rebuilding to be done.

My story happens in August and September of 1666. After a winter so cold that the river Thames froze over, it was an exceptionally hot, dry summer. The plague, which had already killed many tens of thousands of people, was getting worse in the hot summer. The plague was a terrible disease which killed people horribly, and there was no easy way to escape it. Nobody was allowed to leave the city of London unless they had a Bill of Health. It cost money to get that important bit of paper, so the poorer people were trapped within the city walls. When somebody got ill, men called Searchers, wearing bird-head masks, were sent into their homes to see if it was the plague. When people died, their bodies were taken away in 'death carts' and dumped into plague pits. The houses where they had died were nailed up with everybody who lived there shut inside for forty days before the doors and windows were opened again. Most of those people died too.

England was at war with both France and Holland at that time. Great sea battles were taking place. Sometimes people in London could hear the guns booming out at sea. Thousands of sailors died in those battles, and the king needed more sailors to replace them. So press gangs were sent out, grabbing men, chaining them and forcing them to become sailors.

It was a violent time to live in London. Criminals could be hung, drawn and quartered, and their heads put on spikes on display at the end of London Bridge. And some criminals were put onto ships and sent to Barbados to work as slaves on sugar plantations.

People still remembered the English Civil War when people supporting government by parliament had killed and beheaded the previous king, Charles the First. There had been many years with no king of England. But in 1660, Parliament had asked the son of that defeated king to come back to England and become the new king. So Charles the Second became king, but parliament and the people were still wary of him, and he was wary of them too.

The Great Fire happens in my story as it is described by Samuel Pepys and another great man, John Evelyn, in their diaries. The wind, the melting lead and glass, the exploding cobbles, the sound of exploding tar and oil, and the efforts of the king and others to put the fire out, are all taken from their records.

The Tower of London was a very important centre of power for the King. It was a fortress, and had been the king of England's fortress since it was first built 600 years before. Important prisoners were kept at the Tower. But the king also kept his crown jewels there; the symbols of his power. He kept lions and other exotic animals in a kind of zoo within the Tower. The mint that made the country's money, and some of the king's soldiers and his armoury of weapons were also kept there, all under the care of the Lord Lieutenant of the Tower. I have been into a small part of what is now called Queen's House, where the Robinson family lived and where the current Resident Governor of the Tower still lives. I've been up onto the lead roof of the White Tower, without trying to climb one of the turrets! And I've met ravens there who have stolen sandwiches and pecked at anything bright they can find. They look you in the eye and seem to know things!